M000306930

And Then There Were Nun

A. M. Huff

Enjoy!
Best always!
A. M. Huff

Copyright © 2020 James M. McCracken

JaMarque Publishing

All rights reserved.

ISBN-13: 978-1-7329347-5-7

This is a work of fiction. Names, characters, places, and incidents are either products of the author's imagination or used fictitiously. Any resemblance to actual events or locales or persons, living or dead, is entirely coincidental.

DEDICATION

To Barbara LaNora Blair
whose encouragement has kept me pushing
forward every time my characters
led me down a dead-end road.

ACKNOWLEDGMENTS

With heartfelt appreciation to Dennis Blakesley, Pamela Cowan, Anthony Huff, Elizabeth Jones, Phyllis Liesegang-Jensen, Michael Anne Maslow and many more whose encouragement has kept me writing.

CONTENTS

Chapter One	1
Chapter Two	3
Chapter Three	18
Chapter Four	42
Chapter Five	62
Chapter Six	83
Chapter Seven	93
Chapter Eight	121
Chapter Nine	130
Chapter Ten	144
Chapter Eleven	165
Chapter Twelve	188
Chapter Thirteen	199
Chapter Fourteen	215

CHAPTER ONE

Rain was pouring down on the streets of downtown Portland, yet people were out in droves for work, shopping or running to catch a bus. Most paid little or no attention to the many disheveled men and women that stood on nearly every corner begging for spare change, but he noticed them all. He stood at a distance watching them, taking note of their demeanor and the sound of their voice, looking for just the right one. He started at Burnside and moved south along 5th Avenue toward the center of downtown. He had eyed many but still had not found the perfect one. Eventually, he reached the corner of SW 6th Avenue and Morrison Street. Standing against the concrete façade of the Wells Fargo building, he stopped to watch an older gentleman who stood on a wooden crate at the entrance to Pioneer Courthouse Square. The old man was reciting Shylock's speech from Shakespeare's Merchant of Venice. The man was not like the other panhandlers. Though dressed in dingy, soiled clothes like the others, this man held himself in an almost regal posture. It was obvious he was an educated man.

He waited until he had heard enough to know this was his guy. Turning the collar of his trench coat up and pulling it closer to his neck, he made his move.

Finished with his speech, the soaking wet orator sat down on his crate and began counting the pennies, nickels, and dimes passersby had tossed into the rain-soaked hat he had placed on the ground in front of him.

"How's business?" the watcher asked.

"It couldn't be better," the orator said in the same booming voice he had used during his speech. "The rain seems to open up people's wallets. Ah, a quarter!" He held it up as though looking to be sure it was real and not a slug. "Say," he said, dropping it back into his hat and eyeing the well-dressed man before him. "You wouldn't happen to have some change you would be willing to donate to a starving actor, would you?"

"How about something better?"

"A better offer? I'm intrigued," the man said and stood up, hat in hand. "Please, I'm all ears." He gave a slight bow.

"How would you like to earn more money than you could make in a year of standing on this corner?"

"I already said, I'm intrigued. Do tell."

"Fine. Come with me."

The man grabbed his crate and walked beside the stranger.

"I have a part I would like you to play."

CHAPTER TWO

"Be safe and have a blessed Thanksgiving. I'll see you a week from Monday," Sister LaNora announced when the final bell stopped ringing. "You are dismissed."

Standing beside her desk at the head of the classroom with her hands tucked beneath the long black scapular of her habit, LaNora felt a deep sense of pride stir in her chest while she watched her fifth-grade pupils grab their books and bags and hurry out the door. This was by far the best group of kids she had ever had the privilege to teach. For the most part, they were all well behaved and polite, something that made her fellow teachers a bit envious.

"No running in the halls," she reminded them but knew there were one or two who would not listen. It was all right. Sister Angelica, the hall monitoring vice-principal, would be on duty and stop them.

Once the room was empty, Sister LaNora began her daily ritual of tidying up. She straightened the rows of desks, picked up scraps of paper and a stray book or two that had slipped from a pupil's backpack or the bookcase. A scrap of paper on the floor beneath a desk in the back of the classroom caught her eye. It was a crumpled page from a notebook. She bent down and picked it up. Continuing her rounds, she unfolded the paper. A smile slipped across her lips as she read it. She recognized the handwriting.

Sister LaNora is too pretty to be a nun.

For sure, was written by another hand beneath it.

"There was a time," she said aloud quietly to herself remembering the younger version of herself. A memory of Luke sprang to the forefront of her mind and a feeling of longing formed deep inside of her bosom. Longing for yesterday when she was a young, teenage girl. She used to wear her long, shiny, brunette hair tied back in a ponytail. Now, her hair was hidden from view beneath her white wimple and long black veil.

When she decided to become a nun, she could have chosen any number of Orders who did not cut their hair or wear a habit, but she wanted the distinction and protection of the old habit. Wearing it would remind her and others that she was dedicated to God. That was why she chose to enter the convent of the Sisters of the Sacred Heart.

"Oh, there you are." Sister Angelica's raspy voice jolted LaNora out of her thoughts. "Are you okay?"

LaNora looked at the elderly nun and folded the piece paper. Tucking it into the pocket of her habit, she nodded with a smile.

"Yes, Sister. I'm fine. What is it?"

"Sister Victoria wanted me to tell you, that you are to accompany her to the Mother House immediately," Angelica reported.

"The Abbey? Why?"

"She didn't say. However, she did say you need to pack for an extended stay."

"But I have class a week from Monday. Did she say how long?"

"No," Angelica said, "She just told me to give you the message and to tell you to hurry."

"Thank you, Sister Angelica," LaNora said and gave a polite nod toward her senior sister. She grabbed her briefcase and the stack of papers from her desk then hurried out of the room.

The two-story convent was situated across a small courtyard from the elementary school. In no time LaNora stood in the center of her small bedroom. The narrow, single bed, neatly made, sat against the wall with its head in the corner. A nightstand with a lamp and a Bible sat beneath the window, between the bed and overstuffed chair. LaNora pulled the paper from her pocket and looked at the writing. A memory flashed in her mind. A memory of when she was called Rebecca.

The Dairy Queen was packed. It was the day before graduation and in-crowd seniors were already celebrating before the big party that night.

Rebecca barely touched her burger and fries. Her long, chestnut hair was pulled back and gathered into a loose ponytail that hung down her thin neck. Her gold-flecked brown eyes teared while she looked across the table at the young man who sat with her. He was handsome. His perfectly coiffed blonde hair, his deep-blue eyes, and his ripped athletic build made him the object of many schoolgirls' envious restroom conversations.

"I don't understand why you want to be a nun," Luke said as though just saying the word left a bitter taste in his mouth.

Rebecca avoided his eyes and looked at his milkshake. Tiny beads of sweat dripped down the side of the cup and formed a ring puddle around the base. She tried not to hear the pain and heartbreak in his deep voice.

"You're making this hard," she said quietly.

"I don't care," he shouted, but the noise in the restaurant drowned him out. "Don't you care how I feel?"

"I do, but I can't ignore my calling."

"Calling? What calling?"

"God's calling."

Luke ran a hand through his hair.

"Hey guys," Gordy said, stopping beside the table and

looking at them. "Why so serious? Lighten up. We're getting sprung tomorrow." He nudged Luke's shoulder.

"Not now, Gordy," Luke said.

"Sure. Sure. You still coming to the party tonight?"

"I don't know, ask her," Luke answered in a flippant tone.

Rebecca looked at Gordy and forced a smile. "Yes, we'll be there."

"Great. See ya' later."

Rebecca watched Gordy walk away.

"You shouldn't lie if you're gonna be a nun," Luke said.

"I wasn't. We are still going, aren't we?"

"Why? So you can keep pretending to be my girl?"

"Don't you want to go with me?"

"Of course I do. I wanted to spend my life with you. Get married someday. Have a family. But evidently what I want doesn't matter to you anymore—if it ever did."

"Of course it does," Rebecca answered. She reached across the table to put her hand on his but he pulled it away.

"Luke, I care about you, I really do. I have ever since grade school. But I can't help that I feel pulled to a different path."

"You don't have to go," Luke said.

"But I do."

"Why?"

Rebecca looked at him and sighed. This was not the first time they had had this conversation. He was the first person she told when she made her decision after Christmas break. No amount of explaining was going to make him understand. It was as if he did not want to.

"When?" he asked.

"The day after graduation."

Luke looked around at his fellow classmates, their smiling faces filled with hope and anticipation.

"I used to look forward to Graduation Day," he said,

turning back to Rebecca. "Thanks for ruining it."

"I never meant to," Rebecca said.

Luke looked at his tray, seemingly to avoid looking at her.

Rebecca could not help feeling torn inside. She had known Luke since grade school. He was the first and only boy she had ever kissed. They went to homecoming and the prom together and though she felt the same urges as other girls, she never crossed the line of chastity; something she knew disappointed him, but he said he was okay to wait until they were married.

"You'll find a nice girl. You'll marry and have a wonderful life," she said, breaking the silence between them.

"Oh, so now you can see the future?" Luke snapped. "I love you, Becca, but obviously it doesn't mean anything to you."

"It does. I love you, too, but I have to do this. Please, try to understand."

Luke looked at her. His eyes were damp with tears but she could see the fire burning inside them from his pain.

"No," he snapped. "I'll never understand."

He jumped to his feet. He took his tray and emptied it into the garbage on his way out of the restaurant.

A knock on her door jolted LaNora back to the present.

"LaNora? Are you ready?" Sister Victoria's voice called from the other side of the door.

LaNora slipped the paper back into her pocket and grabbed her overnight bag from under her bed.

"Almost," she called out while she reached into her closet and grabbed the two long, black, loose-fitting tunics. She stuffed them, hangers and all, into her suitcase then turned her attention to her black scapulars and waist-length black veils. Her current wardrobe was much simpler and plainer than the one she left behind years ago. Grabbing her undergarments and toiletry bag from her dresser, she tossed them into the suitcase and snapped it shut. She opened the door and immediately stepped back in surprise when she saw Victoria still standing there.

"What kept you so long?" Victoria asked. "We're going to be late."

"Late?"

"Yes, now hurry."

"I'm sorry," LaNora apologized.

"Sister Chloe has agreed to drive us to the Mother House. She's waiting for us at the garage."

"Why the urgency?"

"Mother didn't say. She just said to come straight to her office when we arrive."

The ride to the Abbey of the Sacred Heart did not take long. Set at the top of a hill, the Abbey overlooked Beaverton to the south. LaNora remembered how she felt the first time she visited the Abbey as a young girl with her parents. Emerging from the thick, lush green forest to see the sunlight shining on the three-and-a-half story, hundred-year-old building surrounded by a manicured lawn and well-tended flowerbeds took her breath away. It was at that very moment when she first felt the pull deep inside as if she were coming home. Seeing the Abbey come into view took her breath away again.

LaNora held onto her suitcase while she stood at the foot of the front steps and watched Victoria say goodbye to Sister Chloe. Chloe slipped into the driver's seat and turned the car toward the main gate. LaNora watched the car disappear into the forest.

"Are you coming?" Victoria said, sounding impatient.

"Yes," LaNora answered. She tightened her grip on the handle of her suitcase and hurried up the steps of the Abbey.

Ivy clung to the façade of the original center section of

the brick building, nearly covering it completely. The east and west additions were as yet untouched by nature. LaNora looked up at the balcony outside the Abbess' third-floor room on the east wing. She wondered if the Abbess could see the whole Tualatin valley from that vantage point.

"LaNora!" Victoria said sharply. "What is the matter with you?"

"Nothing," came her knee-jerk response. "I'll tell you later."

"Fine, come on."

LaNora smiled and nodded to the older nun who was holding the main door open for them.

"Mother Abbess is waiting for you both in her office. You can leave your bags with me. I'll take them to your cells."

"Thank you, Sister Margaret," Victoria said and set her small suitcase on the floor.

LaNora hesitated a moment, remembering the state of her habits, then set her case beside Victoria's.

The elderly nun closed the front door and smiled at LaNora. "The others are already here and waiting in Mother Abbess' office."

"Others?"

"Don't ask questions, come on," Victoria said, her impatience ringing loud and clear.

From their days in the novitiate, LaNora knew that Victoria hated to be late for anything. Once when she was late for Vespers, Mother Abbess assigned her an hour of meditation but Victoria did two as her punishment. Victoria was harder on herself than their novice mistress or even the Mother Abbess would ever be.

LaNora tucked her hands beneath her scapular and without running, followed Victoria down the long corridor toward the east wing. Abbess Claire's office was at the end overlooking the cloistered garden in the back. Sister Victoria knocked lightly on the door. LaNora looked at the door across the hall. For a split second, she caught her reflection in the glass. But it was the young nineteen-year-old novice LaNora who looked back at her. Her chestnut hair peeked out from the top of her short white veil. The white of her knee-length dress looked bright against her tanned skin. Butterflies in her stomach sprang to life. She could no longer count the number of times she had been summoned to the Abbess' office. No matter how hard she tried, conforming to the rules of a nun was harder than she had imagined. Now, nearly ten years later, the old feeling stirred once again.

"Enter," Abbess Claire's voice called in answer to Victoria's knock.

Victoria opened the door and stepped into the room. LaNora followed.

The office resembled a library. Floor-to-ceiling shelves filled with books lined the two outer walls. At the head of the office, a large wooden desk sat beneath the windows and faced into the room. Six chairs set in two rows of three, four occupied already, sat in front of the desk.

LaNora closed the door behind them and bowed in greeting to Abbess Claire. The Abbess, a short but stout woman, nodded in response. Abbess Claire was an elderly sister but her habit, which covered everything but her face, made it hard to tell just how old she actually was.

"Good, you've arrived. Please, have a seat," Abbess Claire instructed.

LaNora followed Victoria to the two empty chairs in the back row. She quickly sat down in the one nearest the door. She glanced at her sisters and was surprised to see Sister Juanita, the Abbey's mechanic, and Sister Dominica, the Abbey's resident nurse. They were both members of LaNora's novitiate class along with Victoria. The other nun appeared to be fresh out of high school and wore the white habit of a novice. LaNora had met her the day the young girl had entered the Abbey but, at that moment, LaNora could not recall her name. The remaining nun, much to LaNora's surprise, was Sister Abigail, their old novice mistress. She sat in the front row at the opposite end from LaNora and looked less than pleased, which seemed to be her normal expression.

"I've called you all here because I have a mission for the six of you," Abbess Claire began. "This is Mr. William Drummond. He is an attorney. He has some news to share with us."

LaNora jolted when she looked at the partially bald, white-haired man. His face was long and narrow. His blue eyes were nearly hidden under his sagging eyelids. His lips were thin. There was something odd about him, something that did not look right. Something out of place. LaNora dug deep in her memory but could not find the answer.

Mr. Drummond reached into his brown leather briefcase and pulled out a file. The papers were covered in a blue folder, stapled at the top. Standing up, he flipped the cover over and looked at the papers.

LaNora noticed his hands, aged and wrinkled. There was dirt beneath his jagged fingernails. *Another oddity for a person who makes a living working in an office,* she thought.

"Let me begin by saying my client wishes to remain anonymous," he prefaced in a slightly higher-pitched tone than LaNora was expecting for some reason that she did not know. "He has bequeathed his entire estate in eastern Oregon to the Abbey of the Sacred Heart of Oregon. However, there are some rather unusual caveats." The word rolled off his tongue. He kept going. "First, the six of you must make a thorough examination of the property. For that to happen, you will need to stay on the property for two weeks. During that time none of you will be permitted to leave the property. Should any of you leave, you will forfeit the bequest."

"Two weeks! Mother, that's preposterous! I can't be gone—"

Abbess Claire raised a hand and silenced Sister Abigail.

"Please continue," Abbess Claire said to the attorney.

"Thank you. A driver—" Mr. Drummond suddenly

appeared confused. He looked at his papers and flipped over a couple of pages. His panicked expression relaxed. "Mr. Jack Hastings has been arranged to take all of you to the estate in the morning. He will stay on the grounds in the bunkhouse. He is just your driver and not there to interfere with or assist you in your examination of the property. However, the groundskeeper, Noah Talbot, may help you with… whatever you need, I guess. He has a cabin not far from the lodge."

LaNora's suspicions about Mr. Drummond and her uneasiness grew when she noticed he was reading the papers like a script. *What is it?* She tried to remember but her mind was a blank.

"Both men are free to come and go as they please," he continued and looked up. For a brief moment, his eyes met LaNora's and he looked away.

LaNora noticed his hands begin to tremble.

Sister Juanita, the short, plump Spanish nun sitting in front of LaNora raised her hand.

"Yes?" Abbess Claire acknowledged her.

"Where is this uh-estate?" she asked.

Mr. Drummond appeared flustered once more. Again, he consulted his papers. Apparently finding what he was looking for, his expression relaxed.

"The estate is located on a two-hundred-acre parcel in the Blue Mountains of eastern Oregon. It's off the grid. That means the only power source is from solar panels and generators located in and near the lodge. You'll be happy to know there is indoor plumbing. No outhouses. Are there any other questions?"

LaNora noticed his seemingly self-satisfied smirk. She raised her hand.

"Yes," Abbess Claire acknowledged her.

"Why the six of us? I mean, why us specifically?"

"The six of you have been named in the bequeath," he answered, again reading as if from a script. "Sister Abigail, Mistress of Novices; Sister Victoria, Principal of Our Lady of

Hope Elementary School; Sister LaNora, fifth-grade teacher at Our Lady of Hope Elementary School; Sister Juanita, shop teacher at Holy Redeemer; Sister Dominica, nurse; and Sister Grace, novice."

"I haven't been in charge of the novices for years!" Sister Abigail scoffed, pursing her thin lips and looking every bit perturbed.

"That's okay, the job titles aren't important. The courts recognize that positions change," Abbess Claire said.

Abigail made a huffing sound and looked away, toward her right at the bookcase.

"One more thing," Mr. Drummond continued, again reading from the papers. "Should you decide at the end of the inspection period to keep the property, the estate cannot be sold or parceled out. It must remain intact in perpetuity." He stumbled on the last word and then flipped the page over before closing the file. "That's all."

"All?" Sister Abigail scoffed. "This is absurd. Who is this person?"

"As I said, my client wishes to remain anonymous."

"Your client is dead, sir. What does it matter now?"

"Abigail!" Abbess Claire snapped.

"Mother, I want no part of this cloak and dagger game. Besides, we don't need property in eastern Oregon."

"Is that so?" Abbess Claire said and raised an eyebrow. "Sisters, do you all feel that way?"

LaNora shook her head and noticed a slight smile on the Abbess' face.

"I must admit, it is a bit bizarre, but I'm curious," Sister Victoria spoke up.

Victoria always was the cautious one of their novitiate class. At the same time, she never let it get in the way of her accepting a challenge. That is what initially drew LaNora to her and why they became fast friends. LaNora felt comfortable confiding in Victoria about things she could not tell anyone else. She never felt like Victoria judged her or thought of her as the worst sinner on earth. Even though Abigail had drilled into them that forming close attachments to another Sister was strictly forbidden, LaNora could not help it. She and Victoria were best friends.

Abbess Claire turned her gaze to Victoria's right. "Sister Dominica?"

Dominica was the timid one of their class. When the Abbess called on her, Dominica's cheeks immediately flushed red and she lowered her head. "Whatever you ask, I shall do," she answered in a tone just above a whisper.

Abbess Claire nodded and looked at the young novice seated beside Juanita. "What about you, Sister Grace?"

"I, too, will do whatever you say, Mother. You know what is best for the Order."

"Very well," Abbess Claire said. "Sisters, it is true. We have not given any thought to obtaining additional property, especially on the east side of the Cascades. However, as you are all aware, our Order sends our sisters throughout the state of Oregon. Someday we may want to expand and have a Priory in eastern Oregon. Meanwhile, we may have a use for the property as a retreat house. That is why I am directing that the six of you go and make a thorough examination."

"Yes, Mother," five of them answered obediently except Abigail, who pursed her lips even more.

"Very well," Mr. Drummond said and snapped his briefcase closed. "The lodge is fully stocked with supplies. You won't need to bring a thing, just your personal items. The driver will be here at nine. It's about a six-hour trip to the estate. You should be there before sundown tomorrow and your two weeks will begin at that time."

"Thank you, Mr. Drummond. Sister Margaret will show you out."

Mr. Drummond shook Abbess Claire's hand and then slipped back into the hall. LaNora could hear Sister Margaret's voice and then their footsteps faded into the distance in the outer hall.

14

"Mother," Abigail spoke up. "I want it on record that I am against this. I will go as I have taken a vow of obedience but..."

"Duly noted, Sister," Abbess Claire said.

"Mother, what about my class? I'm due back in the classroom on Monday after Thanksgiving," LaNora spoke up.

"I've already asked Sister Lillian to cover for you. As for the rest of you, your duties have also been temporarily reassigned. Sister Victoria, Sister Angelica will be acting principal while you are gone, and Sister Juanita, I've asked Sister Cecilia to cover your classes and the maintenance department in your absence."

"Don't suppose you found anyone to handle the library," Abigail grumbled and shifted in her chair.

"As a matter of fact, I will handle your duties myself. I know how exacting you are in your work." Abbess Claire looked at the clock on the wall. "It's almost time for supper. Please don't be late. You are all excused."

"Thank you, Mother," the six said and took their leave.

In the hall, Victoria nodded to LaNora to hold back and let the others go ahead. Once they were alone, she turned toward LaNora. "What's going on with you?"

"I have a horrible feeling about this," she answered.

"Not this, before that, back at the convent and all the way here. You seemed distracted."

"Oh, that, it was nothing. Just a note a couple of my boys were passing back and forth started me thinking about what might have been."

"What might have been?"

"What my life would have been like had I not become a nun and married Luke."

"Oh," Victoria said and nodded. "I heard some of the other sisters talking about this. There's an old psychological term that suggests happiness declines after seven years in a marriage, but for us, it's seven years after making our final vows."

"What?"

"When we entered the Abbey as postulants, we had the goal of becoming a novice in front of us. Then after becoming a novice, there was the goal of making our simple vows, and then three years later, our final vows. Once that is over, and life settles into a routine, some sisters begin to wonder if they missed out on something better."

"So you think that's what this is?" LaNora asked.

"Yes, it's a small test. The best thing for you to do is pray and keep busy."

"Oh, believe me, I am."

"Good. Because I've heard more than a few have left the Abbey because of it."

"Trust me, I'm not going anywhere," LaNora said but deep inside, she was not so sure. "So, what did you think of that lawyer, Mr. Drummond?" LaNora asked, changing the subject.

"He seemed like your typical lawyer."

"Didn't you find it strange how he always had to read from the papers in his folder?"

"Not really. I've known lots of boys and men like him. If it's not written down then it's not up here," Victoria answered, tapping the side of her head.

LaNora chuckled quietly. "True. But there was something familiar and a little off about him."

"Off?"

"Yes. It's hard to explain but he didn't look right in those clothes."

"Sister LaNora!" Victoria sounded shocked.

"Oh, not like that. I mean, like I've seen him somewhere before but he wasn't wearing a suit and tie," LaNora explained. "I just can't put my finger on it."

They ascended the stairs to the second floor.

"Well, we all have doppelgangers or so I've been told. When I was in high school friends would walk up to me and ask why I snubbed them at the mall the day before. I hadn't been to the mall. They said if it wasn't me, then I had a twin. A few months later, I came face to face with my *twin*. It was eerie how much we looked like each other."

"Maybe you're right. Maybe he just looks like someone else," LaNora said but deep down, she still felt uneasy.

Victoria stopped at the top of the stairs. She turned to face LaNora, her hands hidden beneath her scapular. She had that look in her eyes that seemed to penetrate deep inside LaNora, making LaNora feel uncomfortable.

"You're going through a moment of testing," she said, "so don't read too much into everything."

LaNora opened her mouth to protest but smiled. "All right," she answered. "This strange bequest came at the right time for me, I guess. We best get ready for dinner."

CHAPTER THREE

A minivan waited in front of the Abbey the next morning. Abbess Claire led the six nuns and Sister Margaret down the front steps.

"Good morning, Sisters," a man with short silver hair and a dark, trimmed beard and mustache greeted them. He wore a blue-and-white plaid flannel shirt, and heavy, tan work trousers. When the sisters approached, he dropped his cigarette onto the pavement and crushed it with the toe of his thick-soled boot.

"Morning, mister...?" Mother Claire said and held out her hand.

"Hastings, ma'am. Jack Hastings." He took her hand and gave it a polite shake.

"Well, Mr. Hastings, I hope you can refrain from smoking long enough to get to your destination."

"Ugh," Jack stammered, looking at his six passengers. He tucked his pack of cigarettes into the breast pocket of his shirt. "Sure," he answered. Seeming a bit nervous, he turned back toward the van and opened the passenger door. "Sit anywhere you like," he said and reached for Sister Dominica's bag. She took a step back and pulled her suitcase away.

"Don't worry about your bags," he said. "I'll put them in back."

"It's okay, Sister," Mother Claire said and put her hand on Dominica's shoulder. Dominica set her bag on the sidewalk beside the others.

LaNora watched Mr. Hastings grab the bags, two in each hand, and head around to the back of the van. She could not help but notice his strikingly handsome face. He was much younger than his hair had led her to believe. She looked away fearing she would blush like Dominica.

"Oh!" she said and gasped while she pulled her cell phone from her pocket. "Before we get in, I'd like to get a picture of us beside the van. Mother, would you mind?" She held out her cell phone to Abbess Claire.

"Not at all. Now get close together," the Abbess said while she held the phone out in front of her.

LaNora stood between Dominica and Victoria while the shorter nuns, Juanita, Grace and Sister Abigail lined up in front. They looked straight ahead and smiled. Abbess Claire tapped the screen right when Mr. Hastings bent down in front of them to grab the last of the bags.

"Oh, I'm sorry, Sisters," he apologized.

"I'll take another one," Abbess Claire said and snapped off another shot of the group. She handed the phone to LaNora.

"Thank you, Mother. I'll take several photos while we're away and text you them so you can see what the property is like," she told Mother Abbess.

"Oh, I'm afraid there isn't any cell service out there," Mr. Hastings said.

"There's got to be. There are cell towers everywhere these days," LaNora protested.

"I don't know. That's what I was told," Mr. Hastings said and shook his head.

"Well, I can see them when you return," Abbess Claire said. "You better get in."

LaNora stepped to the side of the van and lifted the hem of her skirt. She ducked her head and climbed into the empty seat beside Victoria in the back, leaving the other two seats in front for Juanita and Grace. Abigail claimed the front passenger seat.

"Now, Abigail," Abbess Claire said through the open window. "You, being the senior sister, are in charge. Take good care of them."

"You can count on me, Mother," Abigail answered. She glanced over her shoulder at the others. "You hear that? I'm in charge," she said.

"Yes, we heard, Sister," Victoria answered for them. She leaned a bit closer to LaNora. "Still a little bitter over being passed over for Mother Abbess, I think."

LaNora quietly chuckled to herself. It was true. Abigail had been skipped over when the election of a new head of the Abbey was held. While LaNora was not directly involved since she had not yet taken her perpetual vows, she had watched with keen interest.

As Novice Mistress, Sister Abigail seemed a shoo-in for the job. She took her duty very seriously and worked hard at it. However, her lack of tact and mercy around the novice's youthful indiscretions must not have gone unnoticed by the voting sisters. LaNora speculated that was the reason why Abigail had been passed over and why she eventually was made the librarian instead.

The minivan rocked and bounced as Mr. Hastings steered it along I-84, heading east out of Portland. LaNora stared out the window at the passing scenery. She kept racking her brain, trying to figure out where she had seen Mr. Drummond before. A scruffy old man in an oversized, dirty coat pushing a shopping cart flashed in her mind.

"That's it!" she said out loud.

"What?" Abigail asked, turning in her seat in the front.

"Oh, forgive me. I was just thinking about something."

"Well, do fill us all in," Abigail said, her tone

sounding as it had back when she was Novice Mistress, haughty and condescending.

"It was just an answer to a puzzle I've been working on since yesterday. Nothing to bore everyone with, really," LaNora answered, saying a quick, silent prayer that Abigail would drop it.

"Well, please remember a nun never raises her voice," Abigail said and turned back toward the windshield.

LaNora felt her body relax and sink a little deeper into her seat.

Victoria leaned a little closer and whispered, "Now, do you mind telling me what that little outburst was about?"

"I remembered where I had seen Mr. Drummond."

"And?"

"At the time, he was a homeless man. I bumped into him a few months back when I was shopping in downtown Portland for some supplies for my class. He was carrying a crate and looked hungry so I gave him a couple of dollars for a burger."

"Oh tell me you didn't. You know the majority of those people will use it for alcohol."

"Yes, but he seemed different," LaNora answered. "But, he didn't strike me as being a lawyer. And our Mr. Drummond seemed more like he was playing a role, like in a play."

"Well, maybe you are mistaken and he just looks like that man. Remember, doppelganger?"

"Yes," LaNora said with a disappointed sigh. She turned back toward the window but then leaned forward and cocked her head to see around Sister Dominica.

"Mr. Hastings," she said from the back of the van.

"Yes, ma'am?" he answered, eyeing her in the rearview mirror.

"Yes, Sister," Abigail corrected him.

Jack shrugged his shoulders but LaNora saw his disgusted expression in the mirror.

"Do you know who our benefactor is?" LaNora asked.

Abigail turned sharply in her seat and looked at LaNora.

"I'm afraid I don't. I was hired by some guy on the phone to drive you all. That's it."

"Surely he must have given you a name. How did he pay you?"

"Sister LaNora!" Abigail snapped. "That is enough. If you have any more questions, I would appreciate it if you would clear them with me first."

"Yes, Sister Abigail," LaNora answered trying to mask her sarcasm.

"Interesting," Victoria said leaning closer to LaNora so her voice would not be heard in the front.

"Very," LaNora agreed.

The constant noise from the van's engine and the jarring from the road began to make LaNora's head hurt. She looked out the window for some distraction.

"The engine sounds a bit off. Don't you think, Mr. Hastings?" Sister Juanita said.

"Aye, that it does, ma'am—I mean, sister," Jack answered.

"Oh my. Do you think we should stop and have a look at it?" Abigail asked, sounding concerned.

"I suppose. We'll stop when we get to The Dalles. You can stretch your legs and I'll have a look under the hood."

"Gracias," Juanita said. "If you need a hand, I'm pretty good with an engine."

LaNora noticed Jack glance at Juanita in his mirror. His expression was skeptical. LaNora expected to hear the usual "let a man take care of it" response but it did not come. Instead, he smiled and turned back to the road ahead.

By the time they reached The Dalles, steam was pouring from beneath the hood. Jack parked the minivan in front of a rustic, western-style building and shut the engine off. The van shimmied and sputtered before it died.

"That was different," Jack said. "I know it's early, but we may be here a while. Why don't all of you go inside and have some lunch."

LaNora looked out the side window and noticed the sign above the main doors, Doc Holiday's Saloon.

"In a bar, Mr. Hastings?" Sister Dominica objected.

"It's also a restaurant," he said.

"It'll be fine," Abigail said. "Come, Sisters."

"If it's alright with you, Sister Abigail, I'd like to see if I can help Mr. Hastings with the vehicle."

"Suit yourself, Sister Juanita. We'll be inside when you're finished."

"Do you want me to order something for you?" LaNora asked her.

"Sure. Just order me whatever you're going to have. I'm not picky."

"Very well," LaNora said. She glanced at Jack who appeared to be eyeing her. Tucking her hands into her sleeves, she quickly followed the other four.

From the outside of the building, LaNora imagined the inside of the saloon would be filled with dusty, rough cowboy-types and scantily clad barmaids. To her surprise, it bore little resemblance to saloons depicted in the movies. Along the wall, running from the front to the back, was an ornately carved, wooden bar. Behind it, on the wall, were shelves filled with bottles of alcoholic beverages of every color above a counter that matched the bar. In the main floor area, there were no booths. Instead, a mixture of round and square cherrywood tables with matching chairs filled the dining space, some of them occupied. LaNora could not help but notice the shocked expressions on some of the patrons' faces when they saw the five of them walk in.

A surprised barkeep came running over to them.

"May I help you, Sisters?" the nervous man asked.

"We'd like a table," Abigail answered in a tone that was more of an order than a request.

"Of course. Right this way."

He started to lead them toward a secluded corner, away from the bar, but Abigail stopped.

"How about this table?" she asked putting her hand on the back of a chair across from the bar.

"Oh." The man looked panicked. "Sure."

"Great, I'll take a shot of whiskey and a beer while we look over the menu. You do have menus, don't you?" Abigail said while she pulled her chair out.

"Yes, yes. Of course. I'll be right back."

LaNora watched the man practically run back to the bar. Before she was able to sit, he was back with the menus and Abigail's order.

"May I get anyone else something to drink?" he asked sounding a bit hesitant.

"I'll have a hot tea," Sister Victoria answered.

"I'll have the same," Dominica said with a nod.

"Make it four, please," LaNora said. "One's for me and the other for Sister Juanita, for when she comes in." She smiled when she saw the bartender's hands tremble while he wrote on a small pad of paper.

"Do you have any Coke?" Sister Grace asked.

"Yes. Yes, we do."

"Then I'll have one of those."

Abigail dropped the shot glass of whiskey into her larger glass of beer. The man's eyes widened in shock and he quickly rushed back to the safety of his bar.

"Really, Sister Abigail," Victoria said, letting her disapproval be known to everyone at the table.

"There is nothing wrong with having a little drink from time to time. Remember Jesus' first miracle?"

"He turned water into wine not whiskey, Sister."

"Alcohol is alcohol," Abigail answered and took a long drink from her glass.

"That poor man," Dominica said, looking at the bartender and shaking her head. "I'm afraid we may have startled him."

"I don't think he's used to a group of nuns coming in here," LaNora said, feeling sorry for him.

When the bartender returned with their drink order, he took their food orders and left them.

LaNora sipped her tea and looked around. She had never been in a bar before and, except for a sip of wine at Mass, she was not much of a drinker. She had heard the rumors about Sister Abigail and her love of drink, so she was not completely surprised or caught off guard when she heard Abigail order another. Still, it was hard to imagine what was going through the minds of the other patrons who were watching.

"How long do you think before we arrive at the property?" Grace asked.

"How should I know," Abigail said sharply, slurring her words slightly.

"That all depends on what Mr. Hastings and Sister Juanita find is wrong with the van," Victoria spoke up.

"Besides, we don't have a clue as to where we are going. Mother didn't give us a map. We're just along for the ride," LaNora said, reminding them they were all in the dark.

"The Blue Mountains are south of Pendleton," Dominica said. "My father used to take us there for the annual roundup rodeo when I was young. It took us a good five hours, so my guess is we have another two hours or so."

Grace smiled and nodded.

"Here we go, Sisters," the man returned carrying a large tray of plates heaped with fries and burgers. He quickly handed them out and retreated to his post at the bar.

Jack and Juanita entered just after Abigail finished the prayer.

"Looks good," Jack said, eyeing their lunches. "I'll have mine at the bar."

Juanita sat down in the empty chair between Dominica and LaNora.

"So, how's the van?" LaNora asked.

"Just a bit overheated but she'll pull through."

"May I get you something more to drink?" the bartender asked.

Juanita looked at the glasses on the table. Her eyes widened at Abigail's half-empty glass of beer.

"No, I'm fine with my tea, for now, thank you," Juanita answered. She shot a surprised look to Victoria and LaNora.

LaNora shook her head and gave a slight shrug.

"What do you think of Mr. Hastings?" Grace asked.

LaNora was surprised by the young nun's tone. It had the same dreamy-eyed quality she heard from some of her students who were crushing on a boy. The fact that Grace was staring across the room at Jack did not go unnoticed by LaNora either.

"He seems nice but a bit rough around the edges. I don't think he's used to a woman knowing her way around an engine, that's for sure," Juanita said with a bit of a laugh. "For a chauffeur, he doesn't seem mechanically knowledgeable in the least."

"I wonder why he was chosen to chauffer us?" LaNora said. She looked across the room at the bar where Jack sat slumped over his drink. "I do hope he doesn't plan on drinking his lunch."

After everyone had finished eating, Abigail paid the bill and the six went out to the minivan. Victoria excused herself to check on the ice chests in the back. Even though Mr. Drummond had stated the lodge was fully stocked, Sister Frances, in the Abbey's kitchen, insisted on sending along the supplies for their Thanksgiving dinner.

"The ice packs in the coolers are still keeping everything cold," she reported when she climbed into the back seat beside LaNora. "But I'd feel better if we were on the road again."

"What's keeping Mr. Hastings?" Abigail said, tilting

her head from side to side while she peered through the windshield.

"I'll check," Juanita offered and before anyone else could respond, returned to the saloon.

Grace climbed into the van and took the seat in front of LaNora. Dominica sat beside her and left room on the end of the seat for Juanita.

"Honestly." Abigail huffed impatiently.

The saloon door opened and Mr. Hastings walked out followed closely by Juanita.

"How many drinks did you have in there?" Abigail asked in a demanding tone when Jack slipped behind the wheel.

"A couple of beers," he answered and looked at her.

"Are you still able to drive?" Abigail said sharply.

"I wouldn't be too quick to cast any stones. I heard what you were drinking in there. A boilermaker drinking nun. I've heard it all now." Jack let out a boisterous laugh.

"Don't worry about me, Mr. Hastings. I know how to hold my liquor."

"I bet you do, Sister. I bet you do."

Jack turned the key and the engine started right up. *It sounded quieter than before,* LaNora thought. She settled back into her seat and said a silent prayer that they would have no more problems before reaching their destination.

While the van sped down the highway, LaNora caught herself reading the signs and milepost markers just in case Mr. Hastings was wrong about his abilities. She pulled out her cell phone to see if it had a signal. It did. She tucked it back into the pocket of her habit and relaxed a bit more.

Once they reached Pendleton, Jack turned the van south along an unnamed highway, or at least LaNora did not see a sign. The rolling hills on either side of the two-lane road were dry and barren. Rusty barbed wire fences that seemed to serve no purpose other than to mark property lines ran alongside the road's edge. Every once in a while, a No

Trespassing sign twisted on its post in the wake of a passing truck or car.

"This looks positively dreadful. Where are the trees?" Victoria lamented.

"Don't worry, ma'am. There're plenty of trees on the estate. You'll see," Jack said.

"I hope so, Mr. Hastings," she answered.

Mile after mile the scenery had not improved. LaNora began to wonder where these promised trees were when Jack turned east on another two-lane road. The van rounded a bend and was soon surrounded by a forest of tall juniper and pine trees.

"What'd I tell ya, Sister," Jack said while the van began to climb.

"You were right, Mr. Hastings. Please keep your eyes on the road."

LaNora agreed with Victoria. The view on her side of the van showed a steep cliff with scarcely any shoulder. It was no secret, she hated heights. Something her students loved to tease her about.

She felt her mood slump. What would Lillian tell her students? Would they be upset they had a substitute? She missed them already.

The van suddenly made a loud clunk and shimmied. LaNora noticed they had begun to slow. Steam poured out from beneath the hood and streamed past the windows on both sides.

"What was that?" Abigail asked and sat forward in her seat.

"It sounded like the radiator," Juanita answered.

"What she said," Jack said.

"We can't be stranded alongside the road out here," Abigail said, her voice a higher pitch than normal, "in the middle of nowhere." She turned from side to side, frantically looking out the windows.

"I haven't seen a car pass us since we turned onto this

road and even before," Grace spoke up.

"Ladies, there's nothing to worry about. We're almost there," Jack said. "I'll just baby it a little and we'll be fine."

A short distance down the road, Jack jerked the wheel sharply and, with the precision of a skilled driver, found the narrow dirt road between two tall pine trees. The van rocked and bounced but continued along the road. Jack took his foot off the accelerator and let gravity take over. It seemed to work. The cloud of steam dissipated when the stress on the engine eased.

LaNora relaxed and looked at the passing scenery. The mid-afternoon sunlight was obscured by the trees which made it feel later than it actually was. A light shone across the road ahead. When they reached the patch of sunlight, she saw a large clearing to the west of the road. In the center of the tall grass, a buck and a doe looked up from their grazing. They quickly took off in the opposite direction away from the noisy van.

"It's absolutely beautiful," LaNora said. She pulled out her phone and quickly snapped a couple of photographs through the side window. "I wish I had the time to do some sketching and painting."

"Who knows. If this place checks out, we may all have the opportunity," Victoria said.

Once they reached the other side of the meadow, the van began to climb another hill. The engine rattled loudly and steam once again bellowed from under the hood.

"Come on." Jack coaxed the van while it choked and sputtered. "You can make it. Just a little further."

"Hey, look over there," Grace said, motioning out her window.

LaNora looked out and noticed a cabin with smoke coming out its stone chimney.

"Is that the groundskeeper's cabin?" Juanita asked.

"No, that's the bunkhouse. I see Noah's built me a fire. Guess I'll have to let him know I won't be staying after all," Jack said.

The announcement that Mr. Hastings would be leaving came as no surprise to LaNora. The van's engine needed looking at, and from what Juanita had said, Mr. Hastings was not the one to do it.

As the van crested the hill, LaNora looked out her window and noticed a cabin set back from the road. Tall pine trees surrounded it.

"Who lives there, Mr. Hastings?" she asked.

"That, ladies, is Noah's cabin," he answered without turning his head to look. "The groundskeeper."

"Does that mean we're close to the estate?" Sister Abigail asked.

"Close," Jack scoffed. "We're on it. Once we turned off the paved road, we entered the estate."

"All of this land?" Abigail said, looking around.

"Yes, ma'am. All of this land is part of the estate. The lodge is just up ahead."

"Oh my," Abigail said.

Nestled against a backdrop of trees, the rustic two-story lodge came into view. Jack pulled the van around the circular driveway and came to a stop in front of the main entrance. He shut off the engine and turned around in his seat.

"Well, ladies, this is it. We're here."

"Oh dear God in Heaven, what have we got ourselves into?" Abigail muttered loud enough for LaNora to hear. "Well, Sisters, let's go see what all the fuss is about."

The six climbed out of the van. LaNora stretched her arms and legs, shaking them to get the blood properly circulating again. She quickly slipped away to the opposite side of the driveway where she could get a picture of the lodge. In the afternoon sunlight, the natural wooden façade gave off a ruddy glow. Four large stone pillars supported an upper deck that ran the length of the structure.

"It's beautiful, don't you think?" Grace said, grinning from ear to ear and looking at the other sisters for agreement.

"Yes, it is," LaNora concurred, returning to the group. She could not help but think that Grace was acting a bit odd. It was almost as though she was proud of the Abbey's gift.

The five sisters followed Abigail up the wide, paved walkway toward what appeared to be the main entrance. Just as they neared the large wooden doors, they opened. A man dressed in a plaid flannel shirt, work jeans, and heavy logging boots walked out and greeted them.

"Welcome to Cougar Creek Lodge," he said, opening his arms and raising his palms as if presenting the estate to them. "I'm Noah Talbot, the groundskeeper here."

Abigail's back straightened. "Just what were you doing inside?" she demanded.

Noah smiled beneath his neatly trimmed dark mustache and beard. "I just finished building a fire in the fireplace to warm the lodge for you. Also, the kitchen is freshly stocked and the beds upstairs have all been turned down."

"Oh!" Abigail gasped, sounding as though Mr. Talbot had just uttered an improper word. "Well, there will be none of that from now on. We can manage on our own."

"Understood," Noah said and gave her a nod. "I'll help Mr. Hastings with the luggage. Excuse me, Sisters."

LaNora felt her pulse pick up and her chest warmed in a way she had not felt in a long time when Noah passed by her. She would have sworn he winked at her but she averted her eyes and looked at the walk instead.

"Come, Sisters," Abigail said, sounding every bit a Head Mistress again.

The foyer was larger than LaNora expected. The rustic exterior made her think the inside would be cozy. Instead, the foyer was wide, with a nine-foot ceiling and large, wooden double doors with glass panes to the left that led into the dining room. Doors on the right opened to a sitting room complete with a stone fireplace, leather sofa, and chairs. Straight in front of them, a staircase as wide as the foyer rose halfway up the wall and then split into two narrower staircases that switched back going up either side.

Abigail led the group to the foot of the stairs and stood on the first step before turning to face the others.

The front doors opened and Mr. Hastings, with a suitcase under each arm and one on each hand, clunked his way into the room.

"Where do you want 'em," he asked.

"Just leave them there," Abigail said, pointing in front of the dining room doors. "We will manage from here."

"Whatever you say, Sister," Jack said and dropped all of the suitcases at once into a pile on the floor.

LaNora bit her lower lip to keep from laughing. It seemed that Mr. Hastings had already figured out Sister Abigail. Her breath caught when Noah appeared in the open doorway, a suitcase in each hand.

"Just throw them over there," Jack instructed on his way out of the door.

"Gotcha," Noah answered. He set the suitcases down gently and then straightened the others before heading back out the door.

"Sisters, take your suitcase and we'll go upstairs to find our cells," Abigail said. She waited for someone to bring her tattered black suitcase to her. Dominica obliged.

LaNora fell into line behind Sister Victoria and they began to ascend the stairs. After seven steps, they reached a landing beneath a large window that overlooked the back of the lodge. LaNora glanced out at the scenery, a large lawn with a forest of trees at its far edge. The sisters turned to the left and followed Abigail up the remaining steps to the second floor.

Abigail walked straight across the hall to the double doors above the foyer. She set her suitcase down and flung the doors open. "I'll take this room," she announced before entering.

LaNora looked inside the room. Light from the setting sun poured into the large bedroom through the French doors that led outside to the upper deck. A cherrywood queen bed had its ornate headboard against the left wall. Two matching nightstands were placed on either side of it. LaNora watched Abigail toss her suitcase carelessly onto the bed. Without checking to make sure it was not going to fall, she walked around the foot of the bed, across the small sitting area with two leather, wingback chairs, to the open door in the corner. LaNora stared in awe at the stone fireplace in front of the chairs.

"I wonder if the other rooms are as lovely as this," LaNora said.

"Well, there's one way to find out," Victoria answered. "Come on. The others headed that way," she nodded toward the left-wing. "Let's go this way."

LaNora took the left side of the hallway while Victoria, the right. They stopped at each door and opened it.

"Linen closet," Victoria announced at the first door. "Bathroom," at the next.

LaNora continued to the first door on the left and opened it. "Bedroom," she said and turned to Victoria who stood by a door directly across the hall.

Victoria opened the door. "Bedroom," Victoria said and smiled while she looked at LaNora. "Well, it looks like you get to be neighbors with Sister Abigail. Lucky you."

"Oh great," LaNora said sounding less than thrilled. "Hope these walls are soundproofed or someone found a cure for her snoring."

Victoria laughed silently.

LaNora turned to take stock of her new cell. The walls were painted light blue. A single bed sat against the wall to the right with the headboard against the outer wall. Beneath a window that looked out at the forest behind the lodge was a child's writing desk. An antique armoire sat against the wall to the left. LaNora opened the door. Immediately the scent of cedar wafted into the bedroom. LaNora took in a deep breath and smiled as a memory of her mother's cedar hope chest flashed in her mind. She took the handful of hangers from the closet rod and lay them on the bed beside the suitcase. While she unpacked, the sound of someone in the next room startled her.

Returning to the hall LaNora found it quiet and empty. The sound of a door closing caused her to look to her left, toward the end of the corridor. There was a door at the end of the hall which led outside, LaNora assumed it was to the deck. Two more doors, one on either side of the hall, piqued her curiosity. Closing her bedroom door, she went to investigate.

She stopped in front of the door to the room next to hers, where she had heard the noise. Her pulse picked up as her hand wrapped around the glass doorknob. She turned her ear toward the door and listened. Silence. Slowly she turned the knob and felt it unlatch. She waited and then jerked the door open as though ripping a band-aid from an injury.

She let out a heavy sigh. "Bedroom," she said aloud and entered. The bedroom was the mirror image of the one she had claimed. The bed sat against the wall to her left with an armoire on the opposite wall. Instead of a desk beneath the window, an overstuffed chair sat in the corner. Nothing appeared to be disturbed so she returned to the hall.

She crossed the hall to the other door and tried to turn the glass knob. "Locked," she said out loud again. She knocked on the door. "Hello?" she said into the door.

There was no response.

"Is anyone in there?" she said a little louder.

Nothing.

She turned her head and pressed her ear against the door.

"I'm over here!"

LaNora jumped and let out a scream while she turned around and fell backward against the wall beside the door to the deck.

"Oh, I'm so sorry," Victoria apologized and put her hand over her mouth.

"It would be more convincing and sincere if you weren't laughing," LaNora said, pressing her hand over her heart.

"I really didn't mean to startle you," Victoria said. "I heard you calling out. So I came to see what was the matter. Who were you talking to?"

"I don't know. I heard someone moving about in the room next to mine and when I came back to the hall I thought I heard a door shut."

"And what did you find?"

"Nothing. The bedroom was empty," she said, nodding her head at the door behind Victoria. "And that door is locked." She said pointing at the door that led outside to the deck.

"What about that door?" Victoria asked, nodding to the door to the right.

"I didn't try it," LaNora said and grabbed the cold doorknob. "Locked as well."

"I see," Victoria said, furrowing her brow. "Well, the others are all downstairs. Sister Abigail has asked you and me to get the kitchen set up and dinner started."

"Asked? Really?" LaNora said with a smirk. She glanced at the locked door again. "I guess we best go then."

The two made their way down the main staircase to the foyer. LaNora noticed a hall to her left.

"I thought you said everyone was downstairs? Where are they?" LaNora asked, looking around.

"Sister Juanita went outside to see if she could help Mr. Hastings with the van. Sister Dominica and Sister Abigail are looking for a room to use as a chapel. The kitchen's this way," Victoria answered and headed toward the swinging door on the right.

"What about Sister Grace?" LaNora asked while she followed.

"I'm not sure. She told Sister Abigail she wanted to take a look around. Maybe she was who you heard upstairs?"

"Possibly, but why didn't she answer me?"

Victoria pushed the door open and entered the kitchen. LaNora followed.

"Impressive," LaNora said while she took stock of their new, fully equipped kitchen. "This is beautiful."

"I'll say," Victoria agreed.

To the right of the door, along the back wall of the lodge was a door to a huge, commercial-size walk-in freezer. Its metal shelves were fully stocked with boxes and wrapped packages of meats and pre-made desserts. Next to the freezer door and centered on the wall were two large commercial stoves, one with six burners and the other with a large flat griddle. Two wall ovens and a microwave oven were built into the wall beside the stoves. A pantry was in the corner. Straight across from the door to the hallway was a Dutch door that led outside. A long counter ran along the outer wall from the door to the corner. A large white-enamel farmhouse sink was positioned beneath a window that overlooked the side yard. On the wall opposite the stoves was a large stainless-steel refrigerator with double doors. In the center of the kitchen was the biggest island that LaNora had ever seen, topped by a slab of white marble quartz. Six stools were neatly tucked beneath the edge facing LaNora.

"This is absolutely beautiful," Victoria said. She walked around the island to the sink, running a hand over the countertop and the upper cabinet doors. "We should have this back at the Abbey."

"Definitely," LaNora agreed. "Oh, the coolers."

Victoria spotted them as well and already started for them.

"How about some tea?" LaNora asked.

"Sure," Victoria answered. "You'll have to hunt for a kettle."

"I'm sure they have one somewhere." LaNora began opening the lower cupboards of the island. The first one stored large pots and pans, the next held baking pans. In the last she found it. After filling it she walked over to the stove and turned one of the six knobs. After two clicks, blue flames sprang from the burner. She set the kettle of water on it.

"Where do you suppose I'd find tea?" she said.

"Check those cupboards there," Victoria said, nodding toward the upper cupboards on the other side of the sink.

LaNora opened the first cupboard doors. Mr. Talbot had been correct. The cupboard was stocked with more food than the six of them could possibly eat in a month, let alone two weeks. She found a box of teabags and returned to the stove just as the kettle began to whistle.

"So what do you make of this place?" Victoria asked as she finished putting the last of the frozen food into the walk-in freezer.

"I don't know yet," LaNora answered. "I know it's silly but I can't shake the feeling that something's not right. Usually, we know who our benefactor is and there's not a dark mystery surrounding it."

"True," Victoria agreed. "But you have to admit, it's beautiful and peaceful here. It would make an excellent place to do quiet reflection and contemplation."

"That's true."

The kitchen door swung open and Juanita entered. LaNora quickly grabbed another cup and teabag.

"Well, Mr. Hastings is headed back to town. He's going to have the van looked at by a *real* mechanic," she said and pursed her lips.

"I'm sure he didn't mean anything by that," Victoria said.

"I wish I could share your optimism. He's been very dismissive toward me since back at The Dalles when I suggested we have someone there look at the engine."

"Really?" LaNora said.

"It was almost as if he didn't want the van fixed."

"Come, now, Sister. I'm sure he's just not used to a woman knowing about these matters," Victoria said.

"Have some tea," LaNora said and held out a cup to Juanita.

"Gracias," Juanita answered. "With Thanksgiving next Thursday, I doubt he'll be able to find anyone to work on it until after the holiday weekend. If he would have listened to me, he could have saved himself a lot of grief and we wouldn't be stranded here."

"Oh dear," LaNora said, suddenly feeling trapped.

"It will be all right," Victoria said. "Besides, we can't leave the property for two weeks anyway or we'll lose the inheritance for the Abbey, remember?"

"I know, it's just nice having it here," Juanita said.

Victoria took a large pot from the island cupboard and started to fill a pot with water.

The kitchen door swung open and Abigail walked into the room.

"So, what are you going to fix for dinner?" she demanded.

"I was going to fix spaghetti, garlic bread, and green salad. We have one of Sister Frances' chocolate cakes for dessert."

"Great," Abigail said. "I'll get us a bottle or two of wine from the wine cellar. Sister Dominica and I found it in the basement."

Before either of the sisters could comment, Abigail left the kitchen.

"I have a bad feeling about this," LaNora said.

"I'm right there with you," Victoria agreed.

A knock on the kitchen's back door startled the three nuns. Victoria, being the closest, unlocked the deadbolt and opened it.

"Sister Dominica?" she greeted her with a puzzled expression. "What are you doing outside? I thought you were with Sister Abigail."

"I was. Until she insisted that I go find Sister Grace."

"Did you?" Juanita asked.

"No. She's nowhere to be seen. I don't understand where she could have gone."

"That insolent child," Juanita said, shaking her head. "She's always wandering off. I must say, if she makes it to vows it will be a miracle."

"Do you think we should tell Mr. Talbot?" LaNora suggested. "I mean, maybe he could be on the watch for her or help us find her if she's lost."

"Maybe we should wait a while before we bother him," Victoria said. "I'm sure she'll turn up before dinner."

"I suppose you're right," LaNora said and turned toward Dominica. "Would you care for some tea?"

"That would be wonderful," Dominica said.

Victoria let the sauce simmer and joined the other three at the island.

"Did you know there is a hot tub out back?" Dominica said.

"Really?" LaNora said.

"Oh, I wish I would have known. I would have brought a bathing suit," Victoria lamented. "It's been eons since I relaxed in one of those."

"We still can," Juanita said.

"And wear what?" Victoria questioned.

"Our undergarments," Juanita explained. "We can wait until after sundown. No one will see us."

"What about that Mr. Talbot?" LaNora asked.

"He'll be in his cabin. Besides, we'll have towels and robes nearby." Juanita grinned.

LaNora began to daydream about sitting back and relaxing in the hot water. She could almost feel the jets and tiny bubbles massaging her back and shoulders.

"Sister Abigail will never go for it, so we might as well not let ourselves get carried away," Victoria said, snuffing out the dream.

"You're probably right," LaNora agreed. "She tends to be by the book when it comes to the things we want to do."

"But not to what she wants," Juanita said.

The three took one last sip from their cups before putting them in the sink. Victoria checked the pots on the stove.

"These should be fine while we are in evening prayer," she said and followed the three out of the kitchen. When they reached the foyer, Sister Abigail came out of the sitting room with a bottle of Jack Daniel's tucked safely under her arm.

"What?" she said when she looked at their faces.

"The wine?" Victoria asked.

"Oh, I forgot," she said and looked at Dominica. "You can pick out the wine for dinner."

"What about Sister Grace?" LaNora spoke up. "Did you see her?"

"No. I'm going to go up to my room and get settled in," Abigail said.

"But what about evening prayer?" Dominica asked.

"I'm too tired. Go ahead without me this evening."

"Should I bring you dinner?" Victoria offered.

"That would be nice," Abigail said when she reached the landing.

"I think she has her dinner already," Juanita whispered to LaNora. The two shared a quiet giggle.

"What's everyone looking at?"

LaNora and the other three turned around. Sister Grace stood in front of the front doors, a bottle of wine in each hand.

"Where have you been?" Dominica snapped at her.

"I was having a look around outside."

"Really?" Dominica questioned. "I was outside looking everywhere for you. I didn't see you."

"And where did you get that?" Juanita asked.

Grace looked at the bottles in her hands and smiled. "Did you know there is a wine cellar here? Well, in the basement. It has crates of Jack Daniels and a bunch of other beverages, too."

"You can give those to me," Victoria said, reaching

out her hand and taking the bottles from Grace. "I'll put them in the kitchen and meet you in the sitting room for evening prayer."

CHAPTER FOUR

Without the church bells or the bells in the Abbey's tower to wake her, LaNora woke the next morning to the sound of a knock on her door.

"Yes?" she answered, still stuck between awake and sleep.

The door opened and Sister Victoria stepped into the room, fully dressed in her habit.

"I thought I should wake you before I headed down to the kitchen. I figured you'd want to get a shower before the others woke up. I'm not sure how much hot water there will be," she said.

"What time is it?" LaNora asked.

"It's a little past five," Victoria answered. "You best hurry."

"Five," LaNora said and groaned.

"Yes, five, and if you don't hurry up, the others will be awake," Victoria said.

"Thank you. Yes, a shower would be great. I'll be right down after," LaNora said. She could feel the fog of slumber lifting.

"Splendid. I'll be in the kitchen with the coffee ready."

Victoria left the room, closing the door behind her.

LaNora threw the quilt back and sat up on the edge of the twin bed. The floor felt like ice against her bare feet. She pulled them up and then gently eased them down again and stood. She tiptoed the few steps to the armoire. Grabbing her bathrobe and toiletry bag, she headed up the hall to the bathroom.

The cold air in the hall penetrated her long bathrobe and nightgown. Quietly she slipped into the bathroom and started the shower. Steam began to fill the small room and with it, feelings of guilt that the hot water would run out and the others would be forced to take a cold shower set in. She turned the faucet to tepid.

She took the quickest shower she had ever taken since her novitiate days. Back in her room, she dressed and made her bed. Leaving her room, she headed up the hall past the stairs. She paused and knocked on the first door. Juanita responded. At the second door, across the hall from Juanita's room, Dominica, in full habit, opened the door. LaNora proceeded to the door next to Juanita's room and knocked. There was no response. She knocked again a little louder. Still nothing.

"What's the matter?" Dominica asked.

"Sister Grace isn't answering."

"Well, open it. Perhaps there's something wrong."

LaNora opened the door and stood dumbfounded. Grace's room looked untouched. Her bed was still turned down from the night before and was proof it had not been slept in.

"What's the matter?" Juanita asked, walking up to the two. She looked past them into Grace's room. Her hands closed tightly around the towel she held in them. "Not again."

"It doesn't appear she even stayed here last night," LaNora said.

"We'll have to keep a better watch of her," Dominica said.

"I agree. I don't think it's wise for her to be wandering

around. But I'll let you shower. See you downstairs," LaNora said to Juanita.

"I intend to make a full report to Mother Abbess when we get back to the Abbey," Juanita said while she headed for the shower. "Honestly, enough is enough."

LaNora closed the bedroom door and looked at Dominica. She shrugged her shoulders and shook her head.

"Do you think we should say something to Sister Abigail?" Dominica asked.

"No. Let her sleep a bit more. Better to tell her after she's fully rested than wake her with bad news."

When they reached the foyer, the aroma of freshly brewed coffee mixed with the scent of cooking sausage and pancakes greeted them.

"Oh, my," Dominica said in a reminiscent tone. "That brings back memories."

"Memories?" LaNora asked.

"We used to go camping when I was a young girl. My mom would wake us every morning with pancakes and sausage." She smiled and closed her eyes. "That is one of the happiest moments from my childhood."

"I never knew that about you," LaNora said. "Was it just the three of you?"

"Oh, heaven's no. It was my mother and father plus seven of us kids. Being the second to the youngest, I wasn't allowed to help mother with the cooking. Only my oldest sister was."

"Well, this is a fascinating turn to this trip. Getting to know each other better," LaNora said. "My father took my brother and sister and me hunting with him each year. The four of us camped out in a tent for a whole week."

"What about your mother?"

"She wasn't the camping sort. Said if God intended for us to sleep on the ground he wouldn't have created beds with mattresses. She has some strange ideas," LaNora said and laughed.

44

Entering the kitchen, LaNora and Dominica paused and each took a deep breath.

"Smells delicious, Sister," Dominica said while she exhaled.

"Thank you," Victoria said, looking up from flipping pancakes on the griddle. She grinned. "I think I've fallen in love with this kitchen. It's such a treat to have everything right here waiting, not having to drag out a portable griddle and finding a space to put it."

"Well, maybe we could ask Father to remodel the convent's kitchen when we get back," LaNora said. She helped herself to a cup of coffee from the urn at the end of the island.

"Don't count on it," Victoria said. "He's already trying to figure out how to get enough money to fix the roof on the rectory."

"I know, but a girl can still dream, can't she?"

"Dreams are a waste of time, Sister," Victoria said. "They only lead to disappointment."

"Sounds like you know from experience," Sister Dominica said from her seat on a stool at the island.

"I've had my share, it's true. But such are the things of a child. Speaking of children, how is Sister Grace this morning?"

"You mean she hasn't been down this morning?" LaNora said.

"No. At least I haven't seen her. Why?" Victoria asked.

"She wasn't in her room and her bed is untouched."

"Really?" Victoria said, taking a platter from the cupboard.

"Yes," LaNora said.

"I tell you, something isn't right with that girl," Dominica said.

"She's young. You remember those days?" Victoria said.

"I was never that curious to go wandering around

unfamiliar places," Dominica said and took a sip of her coffee.

"Nor was I," LaNora said.

"Well, I'm sure she'll be fine. I mean, what trouble could she possibly get into out here?"

"I guess you're right. But I think we should keep her on a tighter leash if you know what I mean."

Victoria grinned. "Yes, I do and I agree."

The kitchen door opened and Sister Abigail walked into the room. She dropped an empty Jack Daniels bottle into the garbage bin beside the back door and then headed for the coffee urn.

"Good morning, Sister Abigail. Sleep well?" LaNora said.

Abigail grimaced and held up her hand to silence her. She finished pouring herself a cup of coffee and took a sip. Opening her eyes wide and then blinking them a few times, her expression appeared to relax and she seemed to be more awake.

"I suppose," she answered LaNora and then turned toward Victoria. "Is breakfast about ready?"

"Yes, almost. Sisters, would you set the table, please?"

"Yes." LaNora set her coffee cup on the island and grabbed a stack of plates from the cupboard and a handful of flatware from a drawer. She pushed through another swinging door into the dining room. Dominica followed with napkins and glasses for juice and milk.

A large, cherrywood dining table that sat twelve was in the center of the large room. LaNora was still struck by the beauty of the dining room set and matching cherrywood sideboard that was placed against the wall beneath a large antique mirror.

"We'll use the same seats that we did last night. Three on this side and three on that," she said to Dominica.

Abigail entered and stopped cold. She eyed the table and place settings.

"As the superior, I shall be sitting at the head of the

table."

LaNora looked at her and then picked up one of the place settings and moved it to the end of the table facing the French doors into the foyer.

"Very good," Abigail said. "You may call the others to breakfast."

"Yes, Sister." LaNora gave her a nod before slipping into the foyer. She closed the door behind her and looked up to heaven. Taking a deep breath, she tightened her jaw until charity replaced her annoyance.

When she reached the foot of the stairs, Juanita appeared on the landing.

"Good, you're here. Any sign of Sister Grace?" LaNora asked.

"No. Isn't she down here?" Juanita said, looking puzzled.

"No."

"I suppose she's off on another one of her wanderings," Juanita answered. "Sister Abigail won't be pleased."

"Sister Abigail is waiting in the dining room for everyone. So we better find her fast."

"I honestly wouldn't know where to begin to look for her," Juanita said.

"Well, when she wanders off at the Abbey, where does she go?" LaNora asked.

"Any place she's not supposed to."

"Well, that certainly doesn't help," LaNora said.

Just then the front door opened and Grace walked into the foyer dressed in a parka and a pair of jeans and boots. A knit cap with dry pine needles stuck in the threads covered her hair.

Juanita gasped. "Where on earth did you get those?"

Grace looked down at her attire. "I found them in the wardrobe in my room."

"Sister Abigail better not see you looking like that.

Come on, I'll take you upstairs and you can change into your habit immediately," Juanita ordered.

"Don't forget to wash your hands and face," LaNora said while the pair headed up the stairs. "We'll be waiting in the dining room."

Dominica rounded the corner, coming from the kitchen, "Was that Sister Grace?"

"Yes," LaNora said and shook her head. "Sister Juanita is with her now."

"Good," Dominica said. "I was dreading having to say anything to Sister Abigail."

"Thankfully, we won't have to."

The two entered the dining room.

"Where's Sister Grace?" Abigail asked from her place at the head of the table.

"She'll be right down. She's washing up," LaNora answered and glanced at Victoria who had a questioning look in her eyes.

"We shan't wait for her," Abigail said. "Please take a seat and we shall say the prayer."

The sisters took their places and Abigail offered prayer.

They had just started to pass the platters of sausage, scrambled eggs, and pancakes around the table when Grace and Juanita entered.

"Sisters, you are late," Abigail said, stating the obvious.

"Forgive me, Sister Abigail, I have no excuse for being late," Juanita said and bowed her head toward her former Novice Mistress. "It will not happen again."

"See that it doesn't. You may be seated."

Juanita directed Grace the empty chair beside LaNora. She then sat down beside her, making sure Grace could not get out. Juanita bowed her head and said a silent prayer.

"A-hem." Abigail pretended to clear her throat.

Grace and Juanita looked at her.

"Aren't you forgetting something, Sister Grace?" Abigail said in a stern tone.

Grace looked at her, platter held over her plate. She looked at the others with a confused expression.

"No, I don't think so," she answered.

"Put that platter down and stand up," Abigail said, tucking her hands into the opposite sleeves of her habit and straightening her back.

Grace did as she was told, still appearing confused.

"I'm sure your Novice Mistress has instructed you on how you should comport yourself when you arrive at a function late?"

Grace smiled. "Yes, she did. But Mother Abbess isn't here. So—"

"I am the superior here," Sister Abigail said sternly.

The smile vanished from Grace's lips and turned into a defiant glare. She walked to the end of the table opposite Sister Abigail and folding her hands in front of her bosom, bowed and knelt down.

"Forgive me, Mo—Sister Abigail," she said. "I have no excuse for my tardiness."

"Very well, I will decide your penance later. You may take your seat."

Grace stood up and once again sat down beside LaNora.

Once everyone had finished their meal, Sister Abigail sat back in her chair.

"We were sent here to inspect the property and give a report to Mother Abbess. After morning prayers, we shall begin our inspection. Sister Juanita, I am entrusting you to keep an eye on Sister Grace. The pair of you can take stock of the property to the south. Sister Victoria and Sister Dominica, you will look to the west."

"What about me," LaNora said.

Sister Abigail looked puzzled. "You clean the dishes. I will be in my room doing private contemplation. I do not wish to be disturbed. You are all dismissed."

LaNora looked at Victoria. "I guess this means we're on our own for morning prayer."

"I think you're right."

The sisters all helped to clear the table and then met back in the dining room for prayer. LaNora went to close the doors to the foyer and noticed Abigail coming from the hall opposite with a bottle tucked securely under her arm. She turned without noticing LaNora and headed up the stairs to her room.

"Private contemplation my foot," LaNora said under her breath and then joined the others.

"Now, Sister, that's not very charitable of you," Victoria said, startling LaNora.

"My guess is she's either hungover or going to get a head start on one, or both."

"Either way, there's nothing we can do but pray for her," Victoria said. "Come on, let's get started."

"Do you think Mother Abbess knows about this?" LaNora asked while the walked over to the sofa.

"I'm sure she does and I have a feeling that's why there's now a lock on the wine cabinet door in the Abbey's sacristy," Victoria said. "We'll have to say an extra Hail Mary for gossiping, you know."

"I figured we would," LaNora answered.

LaNora's mind was not on her prayers. Instead, she recited them by rote, thinking about the others out scouting the property and her being stuck in the lodge doing dishes. *That'll be another two Hail Mary's,* she could hear Victoria say.

When prayers were concluded, the sisters waited for Abigail to dismiss them but Abigail did not come out of her room.

"Well, let's go," Victoria said.

"Grab your cape," Juanita ordered.

"Yes, Sister," Grace answered.

"There will be no wandering off on your own," Juanita

said loud enough for all to hear.

"No, Sister," Grace said while she swung her long, heavy white wool cape around her shoulders. She buttoned it at the top and then gently pulled the end of her short white veil free from under the collar.

"I really wish you could come with us," Victoria said while she donned her own cape.

"I know," LaNora said and glanced over her shoulder at the stairs.

"We won't be long."

LaNora watched them leave before she closed the front door and headed to the kitchen.

Alone in the kitchen, LaNora set to her duties. After scraping the plates, she filled the first basin of the double sink with hot water and soap and then adjusted the faucet, letting it run at a trickle into the other.

A knock at the side door startled her. She quickly dried her hands on the kitchen towel she had found in one of the cupboard drawers and went to answer it.

"Good morning, Mr. Talbot," she greeted upon seeing Noah standing outside.

"Good morning, Sister," he said and nodded. "I don't mean to disturb you."

"Oh, it's okay. I was just washing the dishes. What can I do for you?"

"Nothing. I was just bringing more firewood. It's part of my daily chores. Would it be okay if I stock the caddy in the front room?"

"Sure. I'll open the front door for you."

"I'll meet you there."

LaNora caught herself staring at Noah while he grabbed the handles of the wheelbarrow that was piled high with firewood. When he disappeared around the front corner of the lodge, she quickly closed the door and rushed to the foyer. She opened the front door just as Noah was about to knock.

"Oh, my," LaNora said when she saw the amount of

firewood in Noah's arms. She held the door open for him even though she did not have to, and put her hand over her chest. She could feel her heart beating rapidly beneath her habit.

"I brought enough to stock the caddy in the master bedroom upstairs—"

"Oh, no," LaNora interrupted him. "That won't be necessary. Sister Abigail is in there and she doesn't want to be disturbed."

"Okay, I'll just leave a few extra logs down here in case she needs them."

"That will be fine."

"So, which one are you?"

"Which one? Oh, LaNora, Sister LaNora."

"Well, Sister LaNora, where is everyone?"

"Sister Abigail sent them off to have a look around."

"Why aren't you outside too?"

"I have been assigned kitchen duty," LaNora answered with a sigh.

"Oh." Noah looked at her and frowned. "It's my least favorite job, too."

"Well, I normally wouldn't mind it but I was hoping to be able to look around, too."

"What's stopping you?"

"Besides being assigned to do the dishes, there's no one left to go with except for Sister Abigail and she's shut herself in her room." LaNora glanced up at the ceiling.

"Well, if you need someone to show you around, I would be happy to."

"Really?" LaNora said and smiled. "I have to finish the dishes first."

"I could give you a hand."

LaNora hesitated. The idea of Noah helping her gave her goosebumps and made her heart flutter. She took a deep breath. "I think it can finish up. It won't take very long, ten or fifteen minutes."

"Okay. I'll put the wheelbarrow away and be back to

pick you up then."

"Very well," LaNora said and felt her cheeks heat. She looked down at the floor to avoid looking at Noah. She walked back to the front door and held it open for the groundskeeper.

"See you soon," he said and was gone.

Alone once again, LaNora closed the door. A heavy thud above her head caused her to duck. LaNora looked up at the ceiling. Sister Abigail's room was directly above the foyer. She listened expecting to hear footsteps or some other noise but there was only silence. Quietly she headed up the stairs to check on Abigail. She walked across the hall to the double doors of the master bedroom and was about to knock when she remembered Abigail gave strict orders that she did not to be disturbed.

Surely she would understand the reason for the intrusion. Any normal person would, LaNora silently reasoned. A memory of a time when she was a novice and interrupted Sister Abigail flashed in her mind. *No, Abigail is not a normal person.* LaNora pressed her ear against the door. There was a faint sound of stirring. She even thought she heard gasping sounds but dismissed them as Abigail's snoring.

"The poor thing just dropped her bottle," LaNora whispered to herself and snickered. Turning around she glanced down the hall toward her room. For a moment thought she saw the door across the hall move. She headed toward it. When she reached the door, she carefully tried the doorknob. It was still locked. She knocked lightly on the door.

"Hello?" she said and then turned her ear to the door.

There was no response.

She waited and listened but heard nothing. She hesitated another moment and then headed back down the stairs to the kitchen.

LaNora had no more finished sweeping the floor when there was a light knock on the kitchen door. She quickly removed her apron, hanging it on a hook beside the hall door. Like a nervous schoolgirl going on her first date, she adjusted her habit while she hurried to answer the knock. She opened the kitchen door.

"Ready?" Noah asked.

"Yes, but we shouldn't go too far," LaNora said.

"That's okay."

LaNora closed the door behind her and the two walked across the side lawn toward a path.

"That building there," Noah said, pointing at the large garage-like shed in front of them, "houses the generators that are used in conjunction with the solar panels on the roof of the lodge. They have a gasoline back-up, so should the solar panels fail there will still be power."

"There must be a lot of them in there."

"There are three industrial-sized generators. With today's technology, they aren't all that big. There is also a two-person quad inside and all the tools anyone would need to maintain the generators and quad."

"I see. Does the quad come with the estate?"

Noah gave her a puzzled look. "It belongs to the owner," he answered.

They passed by the side of the shed and continued along a well-worn path.

"See that small, stone building over there?" Again Noah pointed, this time at an old, metal-roofed structure made of large melon-sized stones and mortar. The building was the size of the tool shed her father had when she was a girl. "That is the well and pumphouse. We get all of our water from there. It gets pretty cold here some nights so the owner had a heater installed to make sure the water in the pump doesn't freeze."

"That's smart."

LaNora looked around at the undergrowth. "This is quite a lovely path. Where does it lead?"

"It leads to my cabin."

LaNora stopped. "I think we should go back."

Noah turned around. "But I thought you wanted to look around?"

"I didn't mean I wanted to see your home."

Noah laughed. "I wasn't taking you to my cabin. The path branches off into different directions just ahead."

LaNora hesitated and looked back toward the lodge. It was barely visible through the trees. She wanted to go back but she also wanted to see more. She turned and looked at Noah.

"Okay, let's proceed," she said.

The two walked on.

"May I ask you a question, Mr. Talbot?"

"Sure."

"What would draw a person like you—"

"A person like me?" Noah stopped and looked at her.

"Oh," LaNora said, realizing she may have offended him. "I just meant a handsome young man. What would cause you to want to live in such an isolated place like this?"

"Uh, well," Noah said with a bit of hesitation. "What would cause a person like you to join a convent?"

"Touché, Mr. Talbot," LaNora said and chuckled. "But seriously, you aren't comparing a calling from God to your choice of living like a hermit out here."

"Is it really so different?"

LaNora smiled. It was obvious Noah was not going to answer her question.

They stopped when they reached a fork in the path. Noah's cabin to the left was clearly visible. The rustic unpainted building reminded LaNora of the old west buildings in cowboy movies. A large metal tub hung from a hook beside a small window at the end of the cabin. The wheelbarrow was propped up against a neat stack of firewood across the small, woodchip covered clearing.

"We can go this way," Noah said, steering LaNora to the right, away from his cabin.

LaNora followed.

The woods thickened with more undergrowth. The scent of juniper and pine trees mixed with the damp, musty smell of decaying leaves from deciduous trees and shrubs.

"How long have you lived out here?" LaNora asked to break the silence.

"Oh, about five—no six years." Noah stopped when they reached a clearing.

LaNora looked around. The sight was eerie. Half-burned out tree trunks and scorched ground spread out before them.

"Oh dear, what happened?"

"We had a lightning strike at the top of the hill last year." He pointed to the south. "It sparked a wildfire. The worst of it is on this eastern side of the hill. Luckily it was stopped before it reached the neighbor's cabin."

"Neighbors? Out here?"

"Yes, we do have neighbors. You can see their place right between those two tall pine trees there." Noah stepped behind LaNora and put his hand on her shoulder. With his other hand, he pointed over her shoulder at the trees. LaNora bent her head slightly and followed his arm to where he was pointing.

"Ah, that's close," she said, but only saw a tall barn structure.

"Yes. But far enough away to give the owner and guests privacy."

"Does it happen very often?" LaNora asked.

"Does what happen?" Noah asked sounding confused.

"The fire."

"Ah," Noah said and returned to her side. "I don't really know. This was the first one for me, but I hear back in the seventies a wildfire made its way up to the lodge. Nearly took it if it hadn't been for the owner and his hired hands. They all worked non-stop around the clock to save it."

"Oh dear," LaNora sounded worried.

"There's nothing to worry about really. Since then the owner keeps the land cleared around any structures. It reduces the fuel for fires to burn and lowers the risk. Besides, we're past fire season."

"It's good you're so knowledgeable about these matters. I'll have to mention you to Mother Claire."

Again Noah cast her a confused look.

"Well, we should probably be heading back."

"Right," Noah said and led the way.

The walk back to the lodge felt easier than walking away from it. LaNora had not realized that they had been moving up the side of a hill to reach the fire line.

"I want to thank you for showing me around," she said when they reached the kitchen door.

"We should do it again sometime," Noah said.

"That would be nice." LaNora felt nervous, the way she had when she had returned home after her first date with Luke. She knew her parents had been watching from inside and though she wanted to kiss Luke, she knew if she was ever going to be allowed to see him again, she should not. Luke still had leaned in and kissed her cheek. The memory caused LaNora to blush.

She turned around and opened the door.

The lodge was still quiet. The other sisters had not yet returned. LaNora made her way up the stairs. She stopped at Sister Abigail's door and listened. Nothing. *Good, she must still be sleeping.* LaNora continued to her room.

Alone with her thoughts, LaNora could not get the image of Noah or the sound of his voice out of her mind. She picked up her Bible from the nightstand beside the bed. She opened it but her eyes would not focus on the words. She tried to silence her mind so she could pray, but even that did not work. Giving up, she left her room and went down to the kitchen.

While she was descending the stairs, the front door opened.

"I don't know where she went," Juanita said, sounding frustrated. "We were walking along a path, commenting on the scenery. When I turned around, she was gone."

"Did you look for her?" Dominica asked.

"No," Juanita said with as much sarcasm as her accent would allow. "Of course I did."

"What's all this racket about?" a voice from behind LaNora asked.

All of the sisters became silent.

"Well?" Abigail asked, standing on the landing and looking down at the three.

"I'm sorry, Sister, but Sister Grace seems to have run off again," Juanita answered.

"Weren't you supposed to keep an eye on her?"

"Yes, Sister." Juanita's tone sounded a bit like a scolded child.

"Where did you lose her?" Abigail's tone was stern and hinted on accusatory.

"We were walking on a path through the woods. I don't know, we were quite a distance from the lodge. It took me a while to get back here."

"Well, we need to find her."

"But how? I called and called but she wouldn't answer me. I don't understand why she was named in the will."

"Why is that?" Sister Abigail asked.

"Because," Juanita said then hesitated and looked at the others. "Because novices aren't supposed to leave the Abbey."

LaNora stared at Juanita. While it was true, that thought had occurred to LaNora the moment she heard the strange bequest in Mother Abbess' office. She could tell that was not what Juanita wanted to say. She wondered if Juanita had noticed the strange coincidence, too, that they were all members of the same novitiate class.

"Well, who knows the mind of our benefactor," Abigail said dismissively and slowly started down the final steps with her hand holding fast to the handrail. "We need to get out there and find her."

"Should I get Mr. Talbot to help?" LaNora asked. "I'm sure he knows these woods better than any of us."

"Certainly not!" Abigail said. "This matter does not concern outsiders."

LaNora glanced at Victoria who stood silently beside Dominica. Victoria had a look of curiosity in her eyes. LaNora shrugged her shoulders and looked away.

The sound of footsteps in the hall to the right of the stairs made everyone look. Sister Grace entered the foyer.

"Where have you been?" Juanita asked curtly. She walked over to Grace and took her arm, pulling her into the foyer to the rest of the group.

"Let go of me," Grace protested and tried to free her arm.

"Sister Juanita!" Abigail said sternly. "If anyone is going to mete out punishment, as your superior, I will be the one."

Juanita released her grip on Grace's arm and stepped back beside LaNora. She offered no apology.

"Sister Grace," Abigail said, raising her chin and looking down at the novice. "Where have you been?"

"I needed to use the bathroom so I came back here."

"Is that so?" Abigail said more than asked.

"Yes, ask Sister LaNora."

A sudden feeling of electricity shot through LaNora's body while she looked at Grace. LaNora's pulse quickened. She knew better than to lie to a superior but she did not dare tell her the truth.

"Is that so, Sister LaNora?"

There it was, the question. LaNora looked back and forth between Grace and Abigail. Her mind was spinning, searching for a way out of this without getting herself into trouble.

"I don't know, I was in my room," she heard herself answer. When Abigail turned her gaze back to Grace, LaNora felt her tense muscles relax.

"Why didn't you tell Sister Juanita where you were going?" Abigail asked the novice.

"I didn't know I needed to ask permission to use the bathroom."

"You don't, but it would have been—"

Sister Abigail raised her hand, halting Juanita's terse response.

"I think what Sister Juanita was saying is when you are off on an assignment it is best to communicate with each other. That way you won't cause your sisters unnecessary worry."

"I'm sorry, Sister Abigail," Grace said but her tone said the opposite.

"What's done is done. From now on, no more going off alone. Is that understood?" Abigail said and looked at each of the sisters.

"Yes, Sister Abigail," they answered in unison.

"Very well, I think it's about time we started our noon meal, don't you Sister Victoria?"

"Right away, Sister Abigail. Sister LaNora, would you be so kind as to give me a hand in the kitchen?"

"Certainly," LaNora answered, thankful for an excuse to get away from the unpleasant situation in the foyer.

Once they were alone in the kitchen, Victoria handed LaNora an apron.

"You weren't in your room, were you?" Sister Victoria said while she tied the apron strings around her waist.

"Not the whole time," LaNora admitted.

"So, mind telling me where you were?" Victoria took out a large bowl from the cupboard beneath the island.

"While I was finishing the dishes, Mr. Talbot came by to deliver more firewood. He asked where everyone was and then offered to show me around. Sister Abigail was in her room sleeping, so I went with him."

"Do you think that was wise considering your present situation?"

LaNora closed the refrigerator door and faced Victoria. "I guess not, but I wanted to go exploring too."

"I know, but you really shouldn't be alone with him. We don't know anything about him."

"I do know he's kind, thoughtful, and respectful," LaNora said in his defense.

"I'm sure he is," Victoria agreed. "But you know the rules of our order. They are there for our protection, spiritual as well as physical."

"You're right," LaNora said and nodded. "So, I guess I should tell Sister Abigail?"

"No. It will only complicate things. Nothing happened so we don't need to add more drama to this situation. Just promise me you won't do it again."

"Okay, I promise."

CHAPTER FIVE

It was hard for LaNora to stifle her excitement when Abigail assigned her to walk with Victoria at breakfast the next morning. Dominica and Juanita were also paired, leaving Grace behind with Abigail.

"I don't know what good that will do," LaNora whispered to Victoria. "If Sister Abigail shuts herself up in her room again, Sister Grace is as good as gone."

Victoria frowned and tilted her head slightly in agreement.

There was a bit of a nip in the morning air though it was not quite cold enough for LaNora to see her breath.

"So, where shall we go?" LaNora asked, eager to see more of the property.

"Well, yesterday we went that way," Victoria said and nodded her head in the direction across from the lodge. "Honestly, there wasn't much to see."

"Good morning, Sisters," Noah called out as he wheeled another load of firewood around the corner of the lodge toward the front doors.

LaNora smiled and felt a warmth blossom in her chest. "Good morning, Mr. Talbot. More firewood, I see."

"Yes, Sister LaNora. Every morning." He stopped the wheelbarrow in front of the two nuns. "I see you're no longer assigned to do dishes?"

LaNora felt Victoria's eyes looking at her. "No, Sister Grace has that chore today."

"Good. So, you two are off to explore more of the property?"

"Yes, Mr. Talbot," Victoria answered in a colder, more aloof tone.

"Why don't you show her the burn?" Noah suggested.

A sudden rush of fear swept over LaNora. She did not dare look at Victoria. She forced a smile and nodded at Noah. "We just might do that."

"Have a good day," Noah said and began loading his arms with the cut wood from the wheelbarrow.

"Come, Sister," Victoria said in an icy tone. She headed up the driveway, toward the main road. "Last night, why did you tell Sister Abigail you were in your room when you were actually out with Mr. Talbot?"

"The truth is when I returned there was no one else other than Sister Abigail. Sister Grace was not inside. I was afraid that while she was wandering, she may have seen me with Mr. Talbot and if I said she wasn't in the lodge, she would have told Sister Abigail that I had left as well."

"LaNora," Victoria said and shook her head.

"I know, I will come clean with Sister Abigail when we get back. I'm sorry."

There was a long pause before Victoria spoke.

"You might as well show me where you went."

"Okay," LaNora said and nodded. "We took the path."

The two began to retrace LaNora's steps from the day before. LaNora pointed out all the details about the shed and water tower and the groundskeeper's cabin.

"Now which way?" Victoria asked when they reached the fork in the path.

"We went this way," LaNora said, leading Victoria

along the path toward the burned-out portion of the forest. "You know, I've been thinking. Why did Sister Grace lie about being in the lodge when she wasn't? What is she hiding?"

"You have dealt with children for how long? You should know they don't have to have a reason for telling a lie. Just being caught doing what they know they shouldn't is enough," Victoria said.

"True."

When they reached the burn, Victoria seemed less impressed than LaNora had been. She looked around at the hills.

"So, are you still upset with me over going for a walk with Mr. Talbot?" she asked.

"No. Not really." Victoria's tone softened. "It's as I said last night, given your present personal trial, do you think it was wise going off alone with a handsome young man."

"You think he's handsome?" LaNora asked.

Victoria pursed her lips and looked at LaNora. "Please don't pretend you didn't notice."

"All right," LaNora answered like a scolded school girl. "I suppose it wasn't one of my better decisions, but nothing happened. I mean, neither of us crossed any lines and it was all above reproach."

"That, LaNora, is between you and God. But, I am happy to hear that. So, how are you doing? I heard you up during the night."

"I don't know," LaNora admitted. "It has nothing to do with Mr. Talbot, though."

"Oh?"

"I just can't help but. . . Did I ever tell you, just before we made our final vows, I saw a picture in the newspaper? It was Luke and some other men. The article said they were going to the Middle East to work on a construction project. They would be gone for two years."

"No, you never said."

"At the time, I didn't care. I mean, he was part of my

past. The feelings I had for him were long gone."

"So, why do you think it's different now?"

"I honestly don't know."

"The note the boys wrote?"

"No. A few months ago I was reading the newspaper and saw an obituary. It was Luke's. He had died from an illness he contracted while in the Middle East. He never married. Never had any children. Those old feelings came back and I began to wonder if I had been selfish by becoming a nun as he said. I began to think if I had married him instead, maybe he wouldn't have gone away. Then he wouldn't have become sick and he'd still be here."

"Oh, LaNora, I'm so sorry," Victoria said and put her arm around LaNora's shoulders. "But you can't think like that."

"I know, but I can't stop it."

"Have you prayed?"

"Yes, but it does no good. I can't shake the feelings of guilt that it was my fault."

"Those are all part of grieving. You will get through this. Whenever you get those thoughts, try thinking about something else. Because what-ifs are a waste of time."

"I'll try," LaNora said. "I wrote a letter to his parents."

"You did? Are they still around here?"

"No. They retired to Arizona. I found their address online."

"And—" Victoria urged when LaNora went silent.

"They sent me a letter back. They, well, his mother blames me for his death."

"That's ridiculous."

"She said Luke was a changed boy after I left him. He was withdrawn and angry. He threw himself into his work and that took him to the Middle East. She said I took her son away and that someday I'd know what it was like to lose everyone I loved or cared about."

"I'm sorry, but she was way out of line. Everyone has

free will. Luke chose his path in life. It's not your fault."

"The head knows that, but the heart is a tougher sell," LaNora said. She looked at the mountains in the distance and the sky. Clouds had moved in and obscured the sun. "May I ask you a question?"

"Sure."

"You've never wondered what your life would have been like had you not become a nun?"

"Oh, I didn't say that. I have wondered how my life would have turned out had I pursued becoming a chef but I don't linger in the thought. I love my life now. It's more rewarding than I ever imagined."

"How do you stop wondering?"

"I wish there were a simple antidote that worked for everyone, but there's not. What helped me was reminding myself why I wanted to become a nun."

"I'll have to try that."

"And remember to pray. God won't allow you to be tested beyond what you can bear."

"I will," LaNora said.

"Is that a cell tower?" Victoria changed the subject.

"Where?" LaNora looked up the hillside.

"There." Victoria pointed at a tall blackened pole that was taller than the other burned out trees.

"I don't know. Let's go see," LaNora said.

The two left the path and carefully made their way closer to the pole. The ground beneath their feet was still blackened with ash and burnt charcoal. The scent of stale smoke, kicked up by their footsteps, was faint but still detectable.

When they reached the tower, they discovered the large metal box that made it operational had been destroyed by the fire. The tower was dead.

"That is disappointing," Victoria said. She turned away from the tower and looked at the view. "This is why our phones aren't working."

LaNora looked around at the burn pattern. "This is odd."

"What?"

"Look at how the plants and grass have already started to come back elsewhere." She motioned with her hand toward the hillside below them. "But here, around the tower, there's nothing. It's almost as though this was not part of the original burn but—"

"There you go again," Victoria said with a smirk. "Looking for a conspiracy."

"I am not," LaNora insisted. "Take a look. You have to see it, too."

"Perhaps nothing is growing here because they kept the ground around the tower clear."

"Then why did it burn?"

The expression drained from Victoria's face as she took another look at the ground. She took a deep breath and pulled the front of her cape closed.

"We should be getting back to the lodge. I have to start the noon meal."

Once they were safely back on the path, LaNora was the first to speak. "It's hard to believe we'll be spending Thanksgiving here, away from the Abbey."

"I know," Victoria said. "I have always looked forward to the start of the holidays. Helping the other sisters in the Abbey's kitchen with baking. There is where I have my strongest memories of growing up. I'm reminded of when I was a young girl. From Thanksgiving until Christmas was my mother's and my special time. She would bake pies and fruitcakes while I made sugar cookies, snickerdoodles, and chocolate chip cookies. The list grew each year. I baked over two hundred dozen cookies each holiday season."

"My word, what did you do with all of them?" LaNora asked.

"Oh, they were eaten. My father's family had a holiday party each year. A quarter of them went there. Then my mother and I would decorate lunch sacks and fill them with cookies, a slice of fruitcake and a card and take them to the sisters at our parish. They held a holiday soup kitchen for the homeless in our town. They handed them out to their guests."

"Sounds lovely."

"It was. My only regret is after I joined the Abbey my mother eventually quit baking. She tried to do it all on her own but it was too much for her."

"I'm sorry."

Victoria took a deep breath and let it out. "So, you see, we all have things that tug at our hearts."

"True," LaNora agreed. She glanced at Noah's cabin when they reached the fork in the path. "Say, do you think we should invite Mr. Talbot to join us for Thanksgiving dinner? After all, Thanksgiving is about sharing and we could get to know h—this place better."

"I suppose we could but we need to clear it with Sister Abigail first," Victoria said.

"I'll ask her tonight after dinner when she's in a good mood."

The lodge was quiet when LaNora and Victoria entered.

"This is odd," Victoria said while they hung their capes on the hooks on the wall beside the front door. "It's too quiet. Check to see if Sister Grace is in the sitting room."

LaNora glanced in the room and noticed the fire had almost burned itself out. She went inside and put another two logs on it and used the poker to stir the embers. Returning to the foyer, Victoria was coming out of the kitchen.

"The morning dishes weren't cleaned."

"She let the fire nearly go out, too."

"Check upstairs, I'll have a look around down here and get started on those dishes."

LaNora quietly made her way to the second floor, careful not to disturb her former Novice Mistress. She started with Grace's room, it was empty as she had expected, and worked her way toward her room at the other end of the hall.

When LaNora came out of her room, she heard a click like a door latch further down the hall. She went to investigate.

"Sister Grace?" she whispered, careful not to raise her voice enough to disturb Abigail.

She approached the door at the end of the hall. It was still locked. The outside door was also locked. She heard a noise above her head in what she assumed was the attic. She returned to the door on the right and knocked. "Sister Grace?" she repeated.

There was no answer. The rustling over her head ceased as well.

Frustrated, LaNora headed for the stairs. She paused when she reached Abigail's room and pressed her ear against the door. There was silence. Confident that Abigail was sleeping, she went down to the kitchen.

"Anything?" Victoria asked without turning to see who had walked in.

"Nothing, no sign of her," LaNora answered.

"How strange. What about Sister Abigail?"

"She must be asleep. I didn't hear anything when I listened outside her door."

"Well, we won't disturb her. Where could that girl have gone?"

"I have no idea," LaNora said, picking up a dishtowel to dry the breakfast dishes.

"We can let those air dry if you wouldn't mind having a look outside?" Victoria said, stopping LaNora.

"No problem."

"Splendid. I will start lunch," Victoria said.

LaNora hung the dishtowel on its rod at the end of the counter and opened the outside door. The air felt colder than it had a few moments ago. Tucking her arms under her scapular, she scanned the side yard. She thought about checking the back of the lodge but decided to look out front first. The covered porch was nice but provided little protection from the wind that had begun to blow.

"Sister Grace," she called out when she reached the front doors. She listened for a response but there was none.

When she reached the end of the lodge, Juanita and Dominica emerged from the woods.

"Don't tell me," Juanita said and shook her head. "Why did she have to come?"

"We need to find her before Sister Abigail wakes up from her nap," LaNora said.

"How can one person cause so much trouble?" Dominica asked.

"Would you two check out back and meet Sister Victoria in the kitchen? I'm going to check on something."

"We'd be happy to," Dominica answered for the two.

LaNora turned around and quickly made her way back to the path that led to Noah's cabin. Having walked the path twice, she was aware of where she was going and made haste. She reached the fork in the path but this time turned left and stopped.

In the clearing at the end of the cabin, Noah raised his ax over his head and brought it down on a thick piece of wood. He was shirtless, exposing a well-defined chest lightly covered in dark hair, a taut stomach, and bulging biceps. She watched as he swung the ax again and then retrieved the split wood. He stacked it neatly in the pile beside the cabin. Taking a drink from a water bottle, he wiped his forehead. His hair was damp with sweat. He poured some of the water over his head and let it drip down his trimmed beard and mustache. The light caught something that hung from a leather string around his neck causing it to sparkle. LaNora felt her pulse quicken.

Noah looked up and quickly grabbed his shirt from the woodpile.

"I'm sorry, Sister," he apologized while he quickly put it on. "I wasn't expecting anyone."

"It's quite all right, Mr. Talbot," LaNora answered. She felt her cheeks grow warm and feared she was blushing.

"I was just chopping some wood for tomorrow's morning delivery."

"I see," LaNora said as the heat in her face intensified. She had not felt this nervous around a man since her high school days.

"What brings you out here?" he asked while he buttoned his shirt.

"I was wondering if you had seen Sister Grace?"

"Which one is she?"

"She's the one wearing the white habit," LaNora answered.

Noah shook his head. "No, I haven't seen her."

LaNora became confused. "Did you bring firewood today?"

"Yes, I did. I knocked and no one answered, so I let myself in."

"Oh my. Did you see Sister Abigail?"

"Is she the old nun?"

"Yes," LaNora answered and tried not to laugh.

"No. The door at the top of the stairs was closed so I just left a couple of extra pieces of wood downstairs with the rest. Then I left. Is something wrong?"

"No. I mean, yes, but not about the firewood. Sister Grace has a habit of wandering off. We're trying to find her before Sister Abigail wakes from her morning nap."

"I see." Noah took another drink from his water bottle.

"Mr. Talbot—"

"Please, call me, Noah," he said and smiled at her.

She noticed the sparkle in his blue eyes and feelings she had not felt in a long time awoke within her. She looked away.

"Mr. Talbot, Noah, there is a door at the end of the upstairs hall, do you know where it goes?"

"Are you talking about the attic door?"

"It has to be the same," LaNora said and nodded.

"Why do you ask?"

"I heard something in the attic but when I tried the door, it was locked."

"It's always locked. I don't even have a key. The family that lived here had a daughter who died. That was her room."

"Oh, dear. I'm sorry to hear that. But someone or something was stirring up there and when I knocked on the door, it stopped."

"I can check it out if you would like?"

"No, that won't be necessary," LaNora answered, fearful of what Abigail would say if she caught him upstairs.

"Okay," Noah said and looked around. "Is there anything else?"

"I—we, that is Sister Victoria and I, were wondering if you would like to join us for Thanksgiving dinner Thursday?"

"Thanksgiving dinner?" Noah repeated and looked a bit pensive.

"I know it's short notice and you probably already have plans. . ."

"No, no plans for me. I'd be delighted."

"Great. I'll let the sisters know to expect you around three?"

"Okay. Three."

"I guess I should be heading back. Maybe the others have found Sister Grace by now."

"I won't keep you."

"Good afternoon," LaNora said and with more effort than she realized, forced herself to turn away from the groundskeeper. Once her back was to him, she felt the pull release and she hurried back to the lodge.

"Where have you been?" Sister Victoria said when LaNora entered the kitchen through the side door.

"I went to ask Mr. Talbot if he had seen Grace," she answered while she donned her apron.

"LaNora! I thought we talked about this. No more going off alone with him."

"I didn't. I just thought since he delivered more firewood this morning he might have seen her."

"And. . .?"

"He didn't. The lodge was empty when he arrived."

"He came inside?"

"Only to put the firewood in the sitting room, but he said there was no one here. Did Juanita or Dominica find her?"

"No," Victoria said and sighed. "What is going on here?"

"I don't know. But when I was talking with Mr. Talbot, he did mention that the attic used to belong to the daughter of the people who lived here. When she died, they locked the door and no one was allowed up there."

"So?"

"So, when I was upstairs I heard something in the attic."

"You don't think Sister Grace would be up there?" Victoria asked.

"I don't see how. The door was locked and even Mr. Talbot said he doesn't have a key."

"I don't like this."

"Where are Sisters Juanita and Dominica?" LaNora asked.

"They went to freshen up before—"

A shrill scream interrupted Victoria and caused her to drop her ladle into the pot of soup. Removing the pot from the burner, she left it and the kitchen to see what was the cause.

LaNora reached the stairs and took them two at a time until she reached the top.

Juanita slowly backed out of Sister Abigail's room, her hands over her mouth and her body trembling.

"What is it?" LaNora asked.

Juanita did not answer. She continued to back out of the room and stopped only when LaNora grabbed her to keep her from tumbling backward down the stairs.

"Juanita, what's the matter?" she repeated.

"L-l-l-look!"

LaNora turned her head and looked through the opened door.

Abigail lay on her back on the hardwood floor between the bed and the doorway. Her head was turned toward the door. Her eyes were bloodshot and gray, staring blindly at them.

LaNora helped Juanita away from the stairs while Dominica rushed past them into Abigail's room. Victoria followed.

"Dear Mother of God," Victoria gasped and crossed herself. "What happened?"

Dominica looked up from checking for Abigail's pulse. "She's dead."

"But how?" Victoria said.

LaNora noticed Grace standing against the wall at the start of the south hallway.

"Stay with her," LaNora said and handed Juanita over to the novice.

LaNora stepped into the doorway and looked around the room. The front of Abigail's habit appeared damp. There were pieces of a broken wine bottle scattered on the floor, some of its contents had soaked into the small decorative area rug. There was a faint trace of stale urine in the air.

"What happened?" LaNora asked.

"It's too soon to tell," Dominica answered.

LaNora looked at the fireplace while she crossed herself. The firewood caddy was fully stocked. She heard Noah's voice in her mind's ear, "I just left a couple of extra pieces of wood downstairs with the rest."

"Sister, please, help me get her onto the bed," Dominica said.

"Do you think we should? I mean, shouldn't we call the police?" LaNora spoke up.

"We don't have a phone and our cell phones don't have coverage here, remember?" Dominica answered.

"Victoria, please, give me a hand."

"Yes, Sister," Victoria said and bent down to lift Abigail's legs and feet.

Dominica wrapped her arms beneath Abigail's arms and clasped her hands. "On three, we'll lift her up and onto the bed."

"Okay."

LaNora watched as the two sisters lifted their old novice mistress off the floor and gently laid her on the bed. The sound of tapping caught LaNora's attention and she looked at the floor. Several loose black rosary beads bounced and rolled across the floor. She stepped forward and under the guise of straightening Abigail's habit, looked for the long rosary all of them wore looped under their belts on their hip. Abigail's was missing.

Dominica removed Abigail's veil and white wimple. She appeared to be looking with interest at Abigail's neck.

"What is it? What's wrong?" LaNora asked and took short, shallow breaths to avoid breathing in the urine smell.

"I don't know. But see these tiny bruises?"

LaNora leaned over the body to see what Dominica was pointing out. There were several tiny purple dots on Abigail's neck. "Yes," she answered.

"It's not for certain but I think she was strangled."

"Strangled?" Victoria said.

"Yes."

LaNora let out a gasp and took a step back, away from the bed. She put her hand over her mouth. She could feel a lump rising in her throat. She swallowed and tried to calm the feeling of nausea.

"Are you sure?" Victoria asked and looked across the bed at Dominica.

"I'm only a nurse but it's my guess based on these marks," Dominica said. She looked back at Abigail's lifeless body in front of her. "I think we need to get the police here, right away."

"How? Our cell phones don't work here," Victoria said.

"There has to be another way. Until then, we should leave the room and not disturb anything more."

"Couldn't it have been an accident?" LaNora said, still trying to make sense of what happened.

"I seriously doubt it," Dominica said.

LaNora returned to the hall followed by Victoria and Dominica, who closed the door behind them. Turning around, Dominica said, "No one is to enter this room until the police get here. Let's go downstairs."

The five nuns made their way down the stairs and to the kitchen where LaNora washed her hands in the sink. Afterward, Victoria and Dominica did the same.

"How can we get the police? Mr. Hastings took the only vehicle in for repairs," Juanita said.

"Not to mention if we leave the property we will forfeit the bequest," Dominica reminded them.

"Wait, Mr. Talbot might know a way," LaNora spoke up.

"No. We mustn't involve him. For all we know, he could be the one behind this," Victoria said, quickly dismissing the suggestion.

"You're wrong," LaNora said. "He's not that sort of man."

"And you know this because?" Juanita asked.

LaNora looked at the others. Suddenly she felt embarrassed. "Because I talked with him yesterday. We went for a walk and he showed me around a bit. And I talked with him a few minutes ago when we were looking for Sister Grace. He told me that Grace wasn't here when he brought the firewood and that Sister Abigail's door was closed so he didn't bother her."

"And you believed him?" Juanita said.

"Yes, I do. I don't believe he would lie to me," LaNora said and paused. She bit her lower lip and looked at

Victoria. "There's another thing," she said in a tone much like a guilty child, "I sort of invited him to Thanksgiving dinner with us."

"Don't you think you should have run it by Sister Abigail first?" Victoria said in a chastising tone.

"I know, but I got nervous and blurted it out. I'm sorry."

"So what did he say?" Dominica asked.

"He said he would love to join us," LaNora said. "So you see, if he did this, he wouldn't be so quick to accept the invitation."

"Unless the man is a cold-hearted killer." Juanita snapped.

"He's not, I tell you," LaNora said, raising her voice.

"LaNora, that is enough," Victoria said sternly.

"Yes, Sister," she answered in a softer tone.

"Well, we can't leave the property so we will have to figure out another way to get help," Victoria said and looked about the kitchen. "Where's Sister Grace?"

LaNora looked around. Grace had once again disappeared.

"For the love of everything holy, can't we put a leash on her?" Juanita asked, sounding completely exasperated.

"Find her," Victoria ordered.

LaNora shuddered with a sudden chill as she watched Juanita hurry away.

The five nuns sat around the dining table. Each staring at the coffee in their cup. LaNora tried to block the image of Sister Abigail lying on the floor from her mind. This was not the first time she had seen a dead body. That had been when she was ten. Her dad's father had died. They had been an open casket funeral service. She could not remember what he looked like dead. Whenever she thought of him, she remembered him laughing and smoking his pipe. There had been several funerals and dead bodies since then, but this was different.

"We need to decide what to do." Victoria broke their silence.

"I think we should ask Mr. Talbot if he has a telephone or radio or some way to communicate with people," LaNora said.

"Absolutely, not!" Victoria said with the authority of a superior. "We all know it appears Sister Abigail was strangled but what we don't know is who could have done it. I am confident that none of us is responsible. Therefore, we have to rely on ourselves."

"We know we can't leave here because we will lose the estate for the Abbey," Juanita said. "And, we can't we call for help?"

"True," Victoria said and nodded but stopped. "What about the cell tower?"

"What cell tower?" Juanita asked.

LaNora turned to her right to look at her. "When Sister Victoria and I were out exploring we found a cell tower on the property not far from here. It was a casualty from a fire."

"Perhaps you could have a look at it and maybe get it working?" Victoria asked.

"I don't know anything about cell towers," Juanita admitted. "But I could take a look. Perhaps you could show me?"

"Sure," LaNora agreed eagerly. She knew that they would have to pass by Noah's cabin and she was trying to figure out a way to involve him and have it look innocent.

"Okay, we have a plan. Why don't the two of you take a walk up there and check it out," Victoria said.

"Shall I take some tools from the shed?" Juanita said.

"No. Don't take anything with you. We want it to look like we are out exploring the land," Victoria instructed while she escorted the pair to the side door in the kitchen.

When the two reached the shed, Juanita glanced back at the lodge. "Wait," she said. "I know Sister Victoria said not to take anything but it's better to ask forgiveness than permission sometimes. Wait here."

Juanita ducked into the shed. A moment later, she emerged with her hands hidden beneath her cape but LaNora could tell she was carrying something heavy.

"Let's go," Juanita said.

"It's a bit of a hike," LaNora warned as the two started up the path.

"Don't worry about me. In my village in Mexico, we walked everywhere. I'm used to it."

By the time they reached the fork in the path, LaNora still had not figured out a way to alert the groundskeeper. She turned right.

"Was that Mr. Talbot's cabin?" Juanita asked.

LaNora stopped and looked back. "Yes, it was. I still wish we could get him to help us. I know he had nothing to do with what happened to Sister Abigail. I don't understand why Sister Victoria dislikes him so?"

"She's right. Until we know who did this, he's our only suspect. Shall we continue?"

Begrudgingly, LaNora started walking. "Come on. It's this way."

They walked only a few yards when LaNora heard Juanita becoming winded. "Should we rest a bit?"

"A moment," Juanita answered. She shifted the toolbox to her left hand and took a white handkerchief from a pocket in her habit and dabbed the bit of her forehead that was not covered. "I guess I'm a bit out of shape for this."

"Couldn't be the extra weight you are hiding under your cape, could it?" LaNora teased but then regretted her comment when she looked at the plump nun.

"I guess Sister Victoria was right about not taking along any tools," Juanita said and moved her cape to reveal a toolbox the size of two lunch pails.

"So, where did you find Sister Grace?" LaNora said, changing the subject.

"I didn't. I was heading back down to the kitchen

when I saw her come out of Sister Abigail's room."

"Did Sister Grace say what she was doing in there?"

"No. She just looked at me like she had seen a ghost. And once I saw Sister Abigail lying on the floor, I screamed."

The two resumed walking and reached the burned-out tower a few minutes later. Juanita looked all around the base of the structure and then up at the top. She pried the cover off the large metal box at the base and shook her head.

"I don't know anything about cell towers but it appears the fire melted the wires in here and there is some equipment missing from over here." She walked over to a rectangle slab of concrete. The center appeared untouched by the fire. Except for a little fresh dirt, it looked clean. Unlike the soot-covered edges around it.

"This looks recent," Juanita said.

LaNora tried to remember when she and Victoria had been there earlier if anything was there. Surely she would have noticed the untouched concrete.

"My guess is whoever did this wants to make sure we can't repair the tower."

"Well, we tried," LaNora said. She was not surprised but still felt disappointed. It would have been nice to be able to communicate with the outside world again.

The pair made it back to the lodge and reported their findings to the others.

"There has to be another way to communicate," Victoria said while she paced in front of the fireplace in the sitting room.

"There are no telephones here in the lodge," Dominica said.

"What about radios? You know, those two-way radios people used before cell phones."

"I didn't see anything like that," Dominica said and shook her head.

"I still think we should ask Mr. Talbot," LaNora said. "We wouldn't have to let on about what happened. We could tell him that one of the sisters is sick."

"No!" Victoria stopped pacing.

"But he has to have a way, otherwise, how would he get his supplies?"

Victoria looked at LaNora.

"Sister Victoria, I agree, it's not a good idea," Dominica spoke up. "For all we know, he is the one responsible. But what choice do we have?"

"I'm sure I can find out without him getting suspicious. Let me try," LaNora said.

Victoria looked at Juanita. "What about you?"

"I have to agree with Sister Dominica. We have no other option."

"Very well, then," Victoria said. "Sister Dominica, you go with her."

"Begging your pardon, but I think I should go alone," LaNora said, watching while Dominica stood up from her chair.

"Absolutely not!"

"But I think he will talk to me if I'm alone. Sister Dominica will be a distraction to him. He may become suspicious and not give me the information we need." LaNora talked rapidly, trying to come up with an excuse not to have another sister tag along. When she ran out of reasons, she was relieved that Victoria did not immediately say no.

Victoria looked at the faces of the other nuns. She appeared to LaNora to be thinking it over. Finally, Victoria's eyes focused on LaNora. "Very well, it's against my better judgment but as has already been said, we don't have any other options. Go, but be back before dark."

"Yes, Sister," LaNora said and jumped to her feet. She rushed into the foyer and grabbed her cape from one of the many hooks on the wall by the door.

"Sister, remember, not a word about. . ." Victoria cautioned while she stood in the doorway of the sitting room.

"I will. And thank you for trusting me."

"That was never in question."

CHAPTER SIX

LaNora quickly grabbed her cape and slipped out the front door before Victoria could change her mind. The air outside had turned colder. She looked up at the light gray clouds that covered the sky. With a skill that would rival a matador, she threw her cape around her shoulders, buttoned it at the neck and headed for the path.

Her pace slowed once she was alone among the trees. Victoria's order not to divulge anything about Abigail to Noah echoed in her mind. She needed to think of a plan but the closer she came to the groundskeeper's cabin, the less her mind would stay focused. The image of seeing Noah without his shirt, his muscular arms holding his ax with sweat glistening on the dark hair on his chest and abdomen, caused her heart to beat faster. By the time she stood outside the front door of his cabin, she had still had not planned for what she would say. She knocked anyway.

Almost instantly the front door opened. LaNora inhaled sharply. Noah, dressed in a heavy, plaid flannel shirt and blue jeans, was even more handsome than she remembered. When he smiled at her, her legs felt weak and her mind went blank.

"Sister LaNora, what brings you out here?" he asked.

"Uh-uh," LaNora replied while she tried to find the words to say. She forced herself to look away and the words came. "The sisters and I were talking and we had a question we were hoping you could answer."

A gust of wind blew against her back. She shivered and held her cape closed in front of her.

"Would you like to come in?" Noah offered and stepped back.

"That would be nice. It is a bit chilly out."

"It gets that way once the sun starts going down."

LaNora stepped into the cabin. She was struck by how tidy and cozy it was. Along the wall to the left of the door was another door that LaNora assumed led to the bathroom. Beside it was an old wood-burning stove complete with cooktop and oven, next to it was a counter and a sink and at the opposite end a tall but narrow refrigerator. Across the room in the far corner was a neatly made single bed. Under the front window were a leather recliner and side table with a lamp. A bookcase stocked with hardbound books sat against the wall in the corner.

"So this is where you live," she said, still feeling a bit nervous.

"Yes, this is my home sweet home," Noah answered and closed the door. "Would you like to sit down?" He gestured toward the small, round kitchen table and its pair of mismatched chairs.

"That would be great." LaNora sat down in the chair with its back to the front door.

"Would you care for some tea?" Noah asked and looked at the single cupboard above the counter between the stove and sink.

"No, thank you."

"So, to what do I owe the pleasure?" Noah asked and took a seat across the table from LaNora.

"Well, Mr. Talbot—"

"Please, call me Noah."

LaNora looked into Noah's blue eyes and felt her nervousness grow in the pit of her stomach. She smiled and looked away.

"Noah," she said and looked back at him again. "We, that is, the other sisters and I, were wondering if you have a means of communicating with the outside world?"

"You mean like a telephone?" Noah asked and tried not to laugh but it came through in his tone.

"Or a radio?" LaNora said.

"I'm sorry, I don't."

"How do you get your supplies? Groceries?"

"I have an arrangement with a guy who works at a store in Pendleton. He comes by every two weeks with a delivery and I give him my order for the next. It's been that way since the fire took out the cell tower."

"Oh, I see. Do you know when they intend to fix the cell tower?"

"Good question. The only thing that runs slower than the government is the phone company," Noah said with a smirk. "I honestly have no idea. It's been nearly six months already."

LaNora looked down at the table and then her gaze wandered to the floor.

"Is everything okay?" Noah asked.

"When do you expect the delivery guy next?"

"Not for another week. Why? Is there something wrong?" Noah asked.

LaNora could see the concern in his eyes. In her heart, she knew he had nothing to do with what happened to Abigail and that she could trust him, but Victoria was the senior nun and she forbade her from telling him. But it would not be the first time she disobeyed a superior.

"Noah, something terrible has happened."

Noah shifted in his chair and his eyebrows raised slightly. "What is it?"

"Sister Abigail, the elderly one," she clarified before he could ask, "died this morning."

"I'm so sorry. How? Why?"

"We think she may have been murdered."

Noah sat back in his chair and his eyes widened with shock. "Murdered? How?"

"Sister Dominica is a nurse and she thinks Sister Abigail was strangled."

There was a flash of fear in Noah's eyes and his hands began to tremble. "When?" he asked.

"The nearest we could tell, it was sometime this morning while we were on our walk."

"I see," Noah said. His shoulders appeared to lower as he relaxed. "Do you have any idea who did it?"

"No," she answered.

"There's no one here but you Sisters and me."

LaNora's back stiffened. "Well, I can assure you that none of us would do such a thing. It's a mortal sin, an unforgivable sin. We need to get a hold of the police in Pendleton."

Noah shook his head. He jumped to his feet and began to pace. "No, no. This can't be happening." He stopped and looked at her. "You don't think I had anything to do with it, do you?"

"No, I don't."

He looked at her. "But the others do."

"They don't know you. I do and I know you would never do such a thing. You're a good man."

"That won't matter to the cops," Noah said. He shook his head and resumed pacing.

"I'll tell them you were with me. It will be okay," LaNora said, trying to calm him.

"That would be a lie and nuns aren't supposed to lie, right?"

"True but I would if it means keeping you safe."

"They won't believe you," Noah said without breaking

stride. "No. I can't do this again."

"Mr. Talbot, Noah, you're scaring me," LaNora said but she was more concerned than frightened. She stood up in his path. "What's the matter?"

"This can't be happening," he repeated, sounding more and more panicked. "Not again."

LaNora grabbed his arms. "Noah, stop," she said in a tone she used on unruly children on the playground.

Noah froze and looked at her. She could feel his arms trembling.

"It's going to be okay," she said in a gentler tone. "Please, sit down and tell me what is going on."

He shook his head and backed away from her, slipping out of her grasp. He walked over to the refrigerator in the corner and wrapped his arms around himself. He looked frightened. His eyes would not stop looking around the room as though looking for an escape.

LaNora watched him. "Noah, please, what is it?"

He finally looked at her. "I'm not a saint."

"No one said you were. I'm not either."

The corners of his lips curled slightly. "Why are you so nice to me?"

LaNora shrugged her shoulders as if to say, no reason, but deep down she felt something. She would not call it love exactly but she was definitely smitten.

"I'll be honest with you, Sister, I didn't come here for some noble reason. I came here after I was released from prison."

"Prison?" LaNora looked confused.

"Yes, I spent nearly two years behind bars."

"Oh." LaNora suddenly felt nervous. She looked away for a moment.

"It's okay," Noah said. "I get that reaction a lot, especially from prospective employers. It was usually followed with a 'we'll be in touch.' But we both knew they wouldn't. That's why I came here."

"I'm sorry. I was just surprised is all. You don't strike me like someone who would have been in prison."

"Thank you for that. I wish I could say I was an innocent bystander, but I wasn't. I mean, if you knew me back in high school, you wouldn't have liked me. After my parents divorced, I gave up caring about anything and everything. I started smoking pot and moved on to heroin but somehow, I managed to graduate. I got a job right away working in a greenhouse. My boss was a nice guy. He actually seemed to care, and for the first time in a long time, so did I. It wasn't easy, but with his help, I quit the drugs.

"Then, one day at closing time, one of my old buddies pulled up in a new Charger. He said he had just bought it and wanted me to go for a ride with him. I was reluctant at first but it was a very nice car. So, I hopped in. He said he wanted to show me what it would do. We headed down I-5 toward Salem. The next thing I know, some cop with flashing lights is behind us. Instead of pulling over, my buddy floors it. I have to say, I was pretty scared. He was weaving in and out of traffic. We had more than a couple of close calls. I freaked out and screamed at him. That's when he told me to take the black bag out of the passenger door and throw it out the window on the next turn. I found the small leather pouch and recognized it instantly. I started to unzip it but he yelled at me to throw it. So, I did. That's when told me that he didn't actually buy the car, he *borrowed* it.

"The next thing I remember was being cuffed and sitting in the back of a state trooper's car. When I saw the black bag in one of the cop's hands, I still figured I'd be cleared. But my so-called pal turned on me. He told them the bag was mine and he had no idea what was in it. He also told them I forced him to drive."

"How could—"

"He told them there was a gun under the passenger seat. I didn't know it was there. But the cops believed him and so did the court. I was sentenced to four years in prison. I served two and was released because of overcrowding.

"When I called my mom to let her know I was out and to see if I could come home, she told me no and hung up on me. My father was even worse. He began to lecture me and I ended it by hanging up on him. After that, I went to see my old boss. I thought maybe he'd let me have my old job back and possibly stay in the back room of the office trailer. He told me he couldn't. Said it'd be bad for business since I had a record now and his insurance rates blah, blah, blah."

"What did you do?"

"What could I do? I was homeless. To keep from having to spend nights on the street, I did what a lot of cute homeless boys in Portland do. I'm not proud of it, but it's how I survived for two years."

"Oh my," LaNora said and put her hand over her mouth. She felt her heart breaking for Noah. "Weren't you afraid? I mean—"

"At that point in my life, I didn't care."

"Noah, you poor man."

Noah shook his head. "It's okay. I deserved it."

"How can you say that?"

"I wasn't nice to my parents and I wasn't nice to my friends either. I used them as much as they used me."

"But still—" LaNora stopped. "How did you end up here?"

"One day while on the streets, a guy approached me. He was old but decent looking enough and judging from his nice clothes, he had money. He took me to a twenty-four-hour diner and let me order whatever I wanted. While I ate, he said he had something he wanted me to do. I told him I wasn't cheap. He said that money was no problem. He then took me to a motel and got a motel room. He handed me the key. He said if I was there in the morning he'd tell me what he wanted me to do. Then he left.

"I'll admit, I almost left before he returned, but I was tired of living on the street and curious to see if he was for real.

"True to his word, he came back in the morning. He told me that he had a job and that it came with lodging. I couldn't say no. Now, here I am, six years later."

LaNora sat for a moment, taking in all of what the handsome groundskeeper had said.

"So, you see, the cops will look at my record and it'll be case closed all over again."

"No, I'll tell them you didn't do it."

Noah smiled but LaNora could still see the worry and fear in his eyes. "I already told you, they won't believe you."

"I'm a nun. They'll believe me," LaNora said and smiled at him.

Noah smirked and appeared to relax. "So, what do we do?"

"We need to figure out a way to get help."

"I could take the quad and go for help," Noah offered. "It won't make it to Pendleton but maybe at least to cellphone range. I could call my grocery friend, have him get the police."

"What about the neighbors?" LaNora asked.

"They're probably gone for the winter already."

"Okay. Sounds like we have a plan," LaNora said but then she grew worried. "Oh, but what would I tell the others? I mean, I wasn't supposed to tell you about Sister Abigail. Sister Victoria will be so angry with me."

"I'll tell them the truth. Just like I told you."

"No, I couldn't possibly let you do that."

"It's okay. I don't want you to get into any trouble."

LaNora thought for a moment. Even with him telling them about his past and volunteering to go for help, Victoria was still going to be upset, but they had no other option.

Moments later, standing outside the front doors of the lodge, LaNora felt as nervous as she had when she came home from the prom and Luke had walked her to the door. She had known her parents were waiting and possibly watching from inside. Still, when he kissed her, it had been magical. Her whole body felt warm from the inside.

"You can wait in the dining room while I gather the others," LaNora told Noah before opening the front door.

"I was just about to send someone to find you," Victoria said, standing in the doorway to the sitting room with her arms folded over her chest. Behind her, LaNora could see the other sisters.

"I'm sorry," LaNora said and stepped aside to allow Noah to enter.

"What's he doing here?" Victoria's voice raised and she took two steps into the foyer. Her arms came down to her sides and her hands clenched into fists.

"We should all talk," LaNora said before Noah could speak. "It's important."

The anger in Victoria's eyes softened slightly while she looked Noah over. "Very well."

"Sister LaNora, a word," Victoria said and motioned for her to cross over to the stairs.

"Noah, please wait for us in the dining room," LaNora said.

Noah nodded and slipped into the room across the foyer from the sitting room.

"What is this about and why are you calling him by his given name?" Victoria asked.

"He asked me to and he wants to help us but first he wants to explain."

"Explain what?"

"That's for him to say. Please."

Victoria relented and called the other sisters into the dining room. Once everyone was seated, Noah slowly explained his past.

"But I had nothing to do with Sister Abigail's death, I swear," he said.

"That won't be necessary," Victoria said in an icy tone. "How can we be certain you won't take the quad and run off and leave us here instead of getting help?"

Noah looked at her in shock. "I wouldn't do that."

"That's what you say," Dominica said. "But fear makes people do things they normally wouldn't."

"Look, I get that you have no reason to trust me and after what I just told you, even more so, but I'm not a monster. And I sure as hell—pardon me—wouldn't hurt a nun. I was raised a Catholic."

"And that is supposed to comfort us? There are a lot of crimes done by people who claim to be Catholic," Grace said, much to the surprise of the others.

"I'm not one of them," Noah answered and looked directly at the novice.

"Well, if you go, you go. It's your choice. We can't and won't stop you. You don't answer to us and we are not responsible for you," Victoria said.

The image of Pontus Pilate washing his hands while he handed over Jesus to the Jews flashed in LaNora's mind.

"Mr. Hastings should be back by the end of the week. He said he had to get the van to a real mechanic." Juanita looked disgusted. "I could have fixed it if I had the proper tools." She shook her head. "Perhaps when he returns we can get help?"

"That's fine if you want to wait that long," Noah said.

"We should get Sister Abigail's body looked at soon," Dominica said. "For that reason, I vote for Mr. Talbot going."

"I do, too," LaNora said.

"Sisters, we are not voting on this," Victoria said. "As I said, Mr. Talbot is free to do as he chooses."

"Fine, it's settled. I'll leave in the morning."

CHAPTER SEVEN

LaNora quietly stepped into the hallway and closed her bedroom door behind her. It was early. The sun had not risen yet. After a restless night chasing elusive sleep, she decided she might as well get up and start her day early.

When she reached the stairs she heard the sound of boards creaking. She turned around and looked back down the hall. There was nothing there. Slowly she made her way toward the door at the end of the hall, tiptoeing and listening to the sound of someone moving above her. Her pulse quickened. The sound seemed rhythmic. It reminded LaNora of the sound her grandmother's rocking chair made. She took hold of the doorknob. The sound stopped. She tried to turn it. The door was locked. She raised her fist to strike the door but then glanced up the hall when she remembered the others. She looked at the ceiling and tucked her hands beneath the scapular of her habit. She would have to try again later.

The air was chilly when she reached the first floor. She decided to get a pot of coffee brewing before coming back to light the fire in the sitting-room fire. When she approached the kitchen she noticed a light coming from beneath the door. She put her ear to the door and listened. The faint sound of humming eased LaNora's fear and she relaxed. She pushed the door open.

"Good morning, Sister," LaNora whispered loud enough for Victoria to hear but quiet enough so as not to startle her.

Victoria looked up from kneading a batch of dough. "Good morning. I take it you couldn't sleep?"

"No."

"Me, neither," Victoria said, throwing a bit more flour on the island countertop. "I couldn't stop thinking or worrying."

"Worrying?" LaNora said while she sat down on a stool across from Victoria.

"Yes." Victoria continued to knead the dough and then wadded it back into a ball before dropping it into a large metal bowl. "I'm concerned that we're not doing the right thing trusting Mr. Talbot. I know," she held up her floured hands to stop LaNora before she could protest, "he may not be responsible for what happened, but you saw how he was. Can we be sure he'll get us help and not just run?"

"He wouldn't do that," LaNora said but her tone lowered, reflecting a bit of doubt.

"And I'm worried about you, Sister," Victoria continued.

"Me?"

"Yes, you. You are going through a personal crisis right now. You should be spending your time in personal prayer, meditation, and reflection. Not going on walks alone with the groundskeeper."

"It was just that one time."

"And last night? You were gone for over an hour for what should have been a one-minute question."

"I didn't want him to become suspicious—"

"But you ended up telling him, anyway."

"I know," LaNora said and looked down at the countertop. She took a deep breath and let it out. "You're right.

I made a mistake."

"Do you truly believe that?" Victoria questioned while she wiped her hands on a kitchen towel.

LaNora looked at her. "He's a good man. I just know it in my gut."

"You want it to be so, I get that, but none of us truly know him. We don't even know who is giving us this land or why? I mean, normally something like this," she said holding out her arms and glancing up at the ceiling, "is passed on to one's children or family. This is an awful lot to hand over to a bunch of nuns."

"I hadn't thought of that," LaNora said.

A knock at the kitchen door startled both the sisters. They recognized Mr. Talbot through the window in the door. Victoria stopped LaNora with a look before going to answer the door.

"Good morning, Sisters," he greeted them but remained outside.

"Good morning, Mr. Talbot," Victoria said in return.

"I was just getting ready to head out, but there appears to be a problem with the quad."

"A problem?" LaNora said and stood up.

"Please, come in," Victoria said and opened the door wider.

Noah took a step into the kitchen and let Victoria close the door behind him.

"Would you care for some coffee?" Victoria offered.

"Please, if it isn't any trouble," he answered.

LaNora took one of the cups from the cupboard and filled it with the fresh brew. She set it on the island in front of the groundskeeper, careful not to let Victoria see her look at him. She motioned toward the cream and sugar bowls.

"This is fine, thank you," Noah said and took a sip.

"You said there's a problem?" Victoria said.

"It appears that someone has cut the fuel line on the quad."

"Are you sure?" Victoria asked.

Noah looked at her. "Oh yes. The shed reeks of gasoline. I left the doors open to air it out. A spark could destroy the shed and the generators inside. We need those."

"Do you think it was intentional? I mean, could it have happened on its own?" Victoria asked. She covered the ball of dough loosely with a warm, damp cloth.

"No, it was definitely cut. A break like that couldn't have happened on its own."

"Who would do such a thing?" Victoria asked.

"Who knew I was going for help?"

"Just the five of us and you," LaNora answered.

"No!" Victoria snapped. "We are not going to accuse any of our sisters of such a foul deed."

"But—"

"No!" Victoria said.

"I'll still go, but now I'll have to walk out. It will take longer but at least—"

"No, you can't," LaNora blurted.

"Sister?" Victoria said in a tone that told her to be silent. "Mr. Talbot, I think what Sister LaNora means is whoever did this doesn't want you to leave, and now, neither do I. You must stay here with us."

"But—"

"We now know we are not alone. Sister Abigail's death is appearing more and more like it was intentional. We can't risk another person being harmed or worse. We'll just have to wait until Mr. Hastings returns with the van."

"As you wish, Sister." Noah relented.

"Mr. Talbot—"

"Please, call me Noah."

"That would not be appropriate," Victoria said firmly. She looked at LaNora and then back at the groundskeeper. "Would you care to come with me? I have a few questions I'm hoping you can answer for me."

"Sure, I'll do my best," Noah said.

"You may come, too," she said to LaNora.

The three took their coffee mugs and went into the dining room where they sat down at the table. Noah sat across from LaNora and Victoria sat at the head of the table, between them.

"I guess my first question is, do you know who your employer is?" Victoria asked.

Noah looked at them with a curious expression. "No. The older gentleman who hired me never gave me his name and I haven't seen him since the day he handed me a bus ticket to Pendleton."

"Didn't you ask him his name?" Victoria asked.

"Desperate boys like I was back then, in that line of work, don't care about names. It's all about doing the deed and getting paid."

"Oh, I see," Victoria said and looked flustered.

"The only person I've dealt with since I've been here is a man by the name of Rothenberg, Edward Rothenberg. He's the one who met me when I got off the bus. He brought me here and explained the duties of the job. Every two weeks he deposits my paycheck in the bank." Noah looked at Victoria's and LaNora's confused expression. "I take it you haven't met him?"

"No, we haven't," Victoria said. "Our Abbey was notified about this place from the attorney who read us the will."

Noah drew back and looked at her with a confused expression. "What are you talking about?"

"Oh my, you don't know?" Victoria said.

"Know what?"

"Mr. Talbot, I'm sorry but I think your boss died."

"No, he hasn't," Noah scoffed.

"I'm sorry, but his attorney, Mr. Drummond, read us the will. Our Abbey is inheriting this property."

Noah shook his head. "I don't know anything about a will or a Mr. Drummond, but Rothenberg is the name of the owner's attorney."

"Then who is Mr. Drummond?" LaNora asked.

Again, Noah looked confused. He shook his head. "I don't know anyone by that name."

"Perhaps he is another attorney in the same firm?"

Noah looked at Victoria. "Rothenberg has his own office in Pendleton. He works alone."

Victoria turned toward LaNora with a shocked look in her eyes.

"Perhaps you could start at the beginning?" Noah asked.

"Very well," Victoria said and recounted the events that had brought them to the lodge. Noah listened in confused silence.

"I hate to be the one to tell you, but the owner isn't dead. He lives in Arizona with his wife, at least that's what Rothenberg told me."

"What?" LaNora said, her voice raised.

Noah looked sympathetically at her and tilted his head slightly to the side. "I'm sorry but it's true. You've been brought here under false pretense."

"But what about all the supplies?" Victoria asked.

"I received a letter that a group of nuns had rented the lodge for a retreat of some sort and was instructed to get the place ready."

"I knew there was something odd about that Drummond guy," LaNora said. "It was all just a ruse to get us out here."

"But why? Why us?" Victoria asked.

"Remember what I told you about Luke's mother's letter? They live in Arizona," LaNora said. "We need to get out of here."

"We can't." Victoria sounded defeated. "We have to wait until Mr. Hastings returns with the van."

"What letter and who is Luke?" Noah asked.

"It's a long story," Victoria said. "But the Reader's

Digest version is that she threatened to kill everyone who Sister LaNora cares about."

Noah looked at LaNora with surprise mixed with confusion. "Really?"

LaNora nodded and avoided eye contact with him. "We need to get word to Mother Abbess about this hoax right away."

"I know and we will, Sister," Victoria said but sounded and looked preoccupied. Her eyebrows were pinched and her lips were pressed thin. She stared at the center of the table.

"What is it?" LaNora asked.

Victoria looked at Noah. "Mr. Talbot, you said you received a letter with instructions about us?"

"Yes."

"Who was the letter from?"

"Rothenberg, I assumed. I didn't really look at it that closely. He always sends any communication with the supply deliveries."

"Do you still have the letter?" LaNora asked.

"No. I used it to start a fire. I didn't think anything of it. The owner rents out the lodge on occasion. It all seemed normal. I'm sorry."

"It's not your fault, Mr. Talbot, but thank you," Victoria said. "What about these deliveries, how often do you get them?"

"Every two weeks. Joe should be coming a week from this Friday."

"Oh my," Victoria said.

"We can't wait that long," LaNora said.

"I know, Sister," Victoria said, sounding curt. "Let me think while I finish getting breakfast ready." Victoria stood up calmly, pushed her chair back in its place. "You will be joining us for breakfast, Mr. Talbot."

"I—"

"Not a question," she said before disappearing into the

kitchen.

Noah looked at LaNora. "Is she always like that?"

"Like what?" LaNora asked.

"Never mind."

The kitchen filled with the scent of freshly baked cinnamon rolls, brewing coffee, and frying bacon as the rest of the sisters awoke and gathered in the kitchen.

"Good morning, Mr. Talbot," Juanita said when she entered the dining room to set the table. "I thought you would have been gone by now."

"I would have except that someone tampered with the quad."

"Really? Maybe I should have a look."

"I don't think there's anything you can do."

"I don't know about that. I'm pretty good with an engine."

"I'm afraid unless you have another fuel line lying around—"

"Fuel line?" Juanita repeated.

"Someone slashed it last night," LaNora said while she placed the silverware on the table.

"Slashed?" Juanita's eyes grew wide and her mouth gaped. "Who would do such a thing?"

"Exactly," Noah answered.

The door between the kitchen and dining room opened and Sister Victoria and Sister Dominica entered carrying platters filled with steaming food. They placed them in the center of the table before taking their places. The aroma filled the dining room and awoke LaNora's hunger.

"Where is Sister Grace?" Victoria asked when she looked around the table.

"She wasn't in her room so I figured she was already down here."

"She's definitely not," Victoria answered, putting her napkin back on the table beside her plate.

"Before I came down this morning, I heard someone

or something moving in the attic. I tried the door at the end of the hall but it was locked and then the noise quit," LaNora explained.

"Mr. Talbot, do you have a key for that door? None of the keys on the ring we were given seem to work," Victoria said.

"No, I'm afraid that is one door I can't open either."

"Why? What's up there?" Dominica asked.

"Mr. Rothenberg told me that it belonged to the owner's daughter who died."

"Rothenberg? Who's he?" Juanita asked.

LaNora looked at Noah and then at Victoria.

Victoria took a deep breath and let it out slowly. "Sisters, we have some news," she said and then informed the other two about what they had learned from Noah.

"So, it was all a lie?" Dominica said with a hint of confusion and shock.

"I'm afraid so," Victoria answered.

"What are we going to do?" Juanita asked.

"Well, first we are going to eat our breakfast and if Sister Grace hasn't returned by the time we are finished, then we shall search for our wandering sister," Victoria answered.

After the prayer, the five ate in silence. When they were finished, Grace had still not returned.

Dominica set the dishes on the counter beside the sink. "So, what's our plan for finding Sister Grace?" she asked.

Victoria scanned the kitchen. The breakfast dishes needed to be washed and the countertops wiped down. "This will have to wait," she said and turned toward the others gathered around the island.

"Do you want me to go look for her?" Juanita asked.

"Yes, but not alone. Take Sister Dominica with you. We'll start inside. I'll check out the first floor and the cellar. Sister LaNora, search upstairs."

"What can I do?" Noah asked.

"Would you mind starting a fire in the sitting room for

us? It's a bit chilly."

"Sure."

"When you are finished, Sister LaNora, meet me in the foyer."

LaNora headed upstairs. When she reached the second floor she made a thorough search of each room. Leaving Sister Abigail's for last. She stood outside the door staring at the doorknob while she debated on whether or not to enter. She pressed her ear to the door. There was nothing but silence. Slowly she opened the door.

Without a fire to heat the room, it was as cold as ice. The dim light from the cloud-covered sky outside offered little in the way of illumination, still, LaNora was able to make out the bed and the form of Abigail's lifeless body. She shivered and looked away. Slowly she walked toward the foot of the bed, feeling the occasional loose bead under her shoes. She opened the doors of the armoire wide and then reached inside to be sure no one was hiding. The only things she felt were Abigail's spare habits that were hung on hangers. She closed the armoire and continued toward the bathroom door. Midway there she bumped into one of the two chairs that were arranged in front of the fireplace. The bathroom was just as Abigail had left it: an empty whiskey bottle in the wastebasket, towels neatly hanging on the rod, and her black toiletry bag beside the sink. LaNora returned to the hall and closed the door behind her. She felt the muscles in her back and neck relax.

"Anything?" Victoria asked from the foyer when LaNora reached the landing.

"Nothing. No sign of her."

"Well, let's hope Sister Dominica and Sister Juanita will have more success. I sent them outside to check the grounds to the south, so we'll head north along the driveway to the main road," she said while she handed LaNora her cape.

"Fire's burning good," Noah announced when he entered the foyer. "Shall I join you?"

"Will it be okay left alone while we're outside?"

Victoria asked.

"Yes. I closed the screen. No worries about a random spark causing a fire."

"Splendid," Victoria said. She took her long black cape from one of the hooks on the wall by the door and put it over her shoulders. "You've been very helpful. Thank you."

"No need. It's my pleasure."

"Yes, you can come with us," LaNora spoke before Victoria had a chance.

Victoria's eyes widened and her lips pursed as she looked sternly at LaNora.

"Great," Noah said.

"Very well," Victoria said. "Let's go."

The air outside was more than just a little nippy. It felt like ice against LaNora's cheeks and nearly took her breath away. She tightened her cape around her neck and tucked her hands beneath it.

"Feels like snow," Noah said. He dug his hands deeper into the pockets of his coat.

"Do you really think so?" LaNora asked.

"Oh yes," Noah said. "And with the quad out of commission, if the snow is like last winter, there's no way I can push a wheelbarrow through it. Perhaps I should bring a few loads of firewood over and stack it outside the front doors?"

"Are you sure that's necessary? I mean, how bad does it snow here?" Victoria asked.

"I'd say the average is around a foot. Last winter it was more like three feet and it hung around for nearly two months. My delivery guy couldn't even make it in."

"What did you do?" LaNora asked, her voice filled with concern.

"I rationed my food to make it stretch. I was down to my last dried up biscuit by the time he finally managed to get through."

"Oh, mercy."

Victoria gave LaNora another look of disapproval.

"Mr. Talbot, please, do bring us more firewood," she said.

"I'll get on it right away. You two will be okay without me?"

"We will be just fine," Victoria said.

Before LaNora could speak, Noah darted off in the direction of his cabin. The two sisters watched him for a moment and then resumed their walk.

"Be careful, Sister," Victoria said.

"What?" LaNora asked, looking around her feet for the cause of Victoria's concern.

"I see the way you look at him," Victoria said as the two reached the gravel of the road.

"I don't look at him in any certain way."

"But you do."

"How?"

"Like a doe-eyed young girl who's about to have her heart broken."

LaNora shook her head and made a dismissive sound.

"You are in a vulnerable place right now, spiritually," Victoria continued. "It would be very easy for your faith to falter and things to get out of control."

"No, Sister, you're wrong about me. I'm okay, honest."

The two reached the bend in the road where it passed by the groundskeeper's cabin. LaNora looked up from the gravel at the same moment Noah stood up from loading his wheelbarrow. For a moment she stopped and their eyes met.

Victoria looked at LaNora then followed her gaze. "Am I?" she said, jolting LaNora away from her vision. "Come on, let's continue walking."

The sound of the gravel crunching beneath their feet was the only thing that broke the silence for the next few yards. LaNora kept thinking about what Victoria had said. It was true, she had developed feelings for Noah, feelings she had not felt since Luke all those years ago. *How could this happen? Why now? Why him?*

"Do you see that?" Victoria said, stopping and grabbing LaNora's arm.

LaNora was jolted out of her thoughts. She pulled against Victoria's touch. "See what?"

"Over there. I thought I saw something like a bright light."

"Where?" LaNora asked, straining to see what Victoria had. She took a step to her right and then left, keeping her eyes focused on the area, and there it was. "That's odd. Should we see what it is?"

"I don't know," Victoria said, sounding a bit uneasy. "I suppose we should, but be careful."

The two continued up the road a few more yards and then stopped.

"I don't remember seeing this when we drove in," LaNora said, looking at the torn-up grass. "It appears that someone went off the road here. Do you think it could have been made by a quad?"

"I don't think so. These look like they were made by a larger vehicle," Victoria answered. "They appear to have gone through there." She gestured between two large juniper trees that had some of their lower branches broken off.

LaNora took her cell phone out of the pocket in her habit. She held it up in the air and looked at the screen.

"Do you have anything?" Victoria asked.

"No. Not a single bar," LaNora answered and slipped the phone back into her pocket.

"Maybe we should go back and get Mr. Talbot," Victoria said.

"But what if it's nothing? We're here. We can see where this goes and if we find anything, then get him."

"Very well, but stay close and be careful," Victoria said as the two left the gravel road and started down the path cut by some sort of motor vehicle through the trees.

LaNora could feel her ankles twisting while she followed Victoria down the gentle slope of the hill. The wide heels of her shoes did not offer much stability on the uneven ground but it was better than walking on the compressed grass of the tire track. Twice she nearly slipped. Returning to walking between the tracks, LaNora kept her eyes focused on the ground.

"Look! Is that the van?" Victoria said, stopping without warning.

"Where?" LaNora asked and slipped when she tried to stop. She bumped into Victoria and regained her balance.

"There," Victoria said, pointing ahead of them.

"Oh dear," LaNora said.

Ahead of them a few yards away was indeed the van. It had come to rest against the trunk of a larger juniper tree.

"Come, Sister, we need to check to see if Mr. Hastings is inside," Victoria said and continued.

They approached the vehicle slowly. A camouflage net had been pulled over the top of the van and tree branches were leaned against its sides in an effort to hide it.

"This was no accident," Victoria said.

LaNora could feel her pulse quicken. The urge to leave pulled at her. She stopped when she reached the rear of the van. "But why?" she said.

Victoria did not answer. She slowly made her way along the side toward the driver's door.

LaNora looked through the back window. The van appeared to be empty.

"LaNora, come here," Victoria said with an urgent tone in her voice.

Ignoring her fear, LaNora inched her way along the side of the van, tossing aside the branches in her way. "What is it?"

"Blood."

"Blood?" LaNora repeated, nearly shouting. She looked through the broken window of the driver's door and saw blood on the deflated airbag. Lots of blood. She looked up at the windshield. It was cracked and spider-webbed but not broken out. Both front tires were flat. "Where is he?"

LaNora looked at the pedals. A broken bottle, its jagged edges covered in blood, lay lodged beneath the brake. She stepped back.

"Sister, look at the brake. Do you think Mr. Hastings was drinking while driving?"

Victoria stepped forward and took a look. She crossed herself and backed away.

"No. This was no accident," she said. "Someone intentionally did this." She stepped back and looked at the netting.

"But where is he?" LaNora asked.

"I don't know," Victoria answered.

"We should get No—Mr. Talbot," LaNora said.

"For once, I have to agree with you."

Returning to the road was a bit more difficult than LaNora had imagined. The hillside was steep. When they finally reached the road, they rested a moment to catch their breath before hurrying down the long driveway to Noah's cabin. It did not take much convincing for him to drop his armful of firewood and follow them. Soon they were all standing beside the crumpled van.

"Where could he have gone?" Victoria asked while Noah looked through the driver's door window.

"There's too much blood," he said and stepped back. "He couldn't have gone anywhere on his own."

"Would a wild animal have. . ." LaNora asked but stopped short of actually verbalizing her fear.

"It's possible but not probable. You said the door was shut when you arrived?"

"Yes," Victoria answered.

"And this netting was here?"

"Yes. We didn't touch anything."

"This was deliberate," Noah said. "Whoever did this

was trying to hide it."

"But who would do such a thing?" Victoria said.

Noah turned back to look at the van again. "What bothers me is from the marks left in the gravel when he went off the road and the dried blood, this must have happened right after he dropped you off. Why didn't we hear it?"

"We were all inside looking over the lodge—"

"Except for Sister Grace," LaNora interrupted Victoria.

"Sister!" Victoria said sharply.

"I wasn't accusing her. I was just thinking she might have heard something."

"Well, there's only one way to find out. We better get you two back to the lodge," Noah said. The sense of urgency in his tone frightened LaNora.

"I think you're right, Mr. Talbot," Victoria said.

By the time the three had reached the driveway, the air had grown colder. Even moving at a slower pace seemed to take their breath away. LaNora pulled her cell phone out again and checked it while they rested a moment.

"Still nothing," she reported and tucked it back into her pocket.

"Well, we'll just have to forget about it for now. Let's go," Victoria said.

A cold wind began to blow and the sky darkened. LaNora held her cape closed in front of her while the three headed back to the lodge.

When they reached Noah's cabin they stopped.

"I should get that firewood," he said. "It looks more and more like we're in for some snow. Wait for me here, I'll only be a second."

While Noah fetched his wheelbarrow, Victoria and LaNora huddled closer to keep warm.

"I can't believe this is happening," LaNora whispered. Her breath made a cloud in front of her face and quickly dissipated. "What are we going to do?"

"Pray, Sister. Pray."

LaNora wished those words felt more comforting. There were times when they had been, but at that moment her fear was stronger than her faith. The sound of a tire on gravel startled her out of her thoughts.

"Okay, Sisters, let's go," Noah said while he pushed the heaping load of firewood past them.

When the lodge came into view, LaNora felt her fears ease slightly and her shoulders relax.

"Do you think Sister Juanita and Sister Dominica found our wandering nun?" she asked.

"I certainly hope so."

When the three reached the front door, Juanita came running around the corner of the lodge.

"Sisters, help!" she screamed.

"What is it?" Victoria asked, rushing toward Juanita.

"It's Sister Dominica. We were searching the woods behind the lodge and she stepped in a trap."

"What sort of trap?" Noah asked.

Juanita looked at him. "You should know."

"No, I don't. We don't use any traps here."

"It looks like an animal trap. It has sharp teeth on it. It clamped on her ankle and I couldn't get it off her. Please, hurry. She's in a lot of pain."

The three followed Juanita. She took them around the lodge to the back and down a path that led south into the woods.

"She thought she saw someone moving in the shadows up ahead," Juanita explained while they moved single file along the path. "I was behind her and didn't see. We're almost there," she said and then raised her voice. "Sister Dominica, we're coming!"

LaNora listened for a reply but there was none. "Dominica!" she called out.

"Sister!" Victoria turned around and gave her a stern look.

"How far is she?" LaNora asked Juanita, ignoring Victoria's reprimand.

"We were just about to the top of this hill," she answered. "But we should be able to see her."

"Were you walking on the path?" Noah asked.

"Yes."

Noah turned and gave LaNora a concerned look.

"There!" Juanita said with a hint of excitement and relief.

LaNora looked in the direction that Juanita had pointed. In the brush, lying motionless on the ground was Dominica. "I thought you said you didn't leave the path?" LaNora said.

"We didn't. She couldn't have made it that far. The trap was anchored to the ground by a short chain and metal spike. I don't understand it."

"Sisters," Noah said and moved to the front of the line. He turned around and halted them. "I think it's best if I go have a look first."

LaNora could see the fear in his eyes and wondered what was causing it. She tried to see behind him, on the path but could not.

"It's best if you stay here, please," he said.

"Why, Mr. Talbot?" Victoria asked in a demanding tone.

"I have a bad feeling about this," he answered but LaNora could sense he was not telling them everything.

"She's our sister," Victoria said.

"Do you know what an animal trap like the one Sister Juanita described does? There's only one way an animal can get out of it and it's not pretty."

"Sister Dominica is not an animal!"

"I know that, Sister. All the more reason to stay put while I check it out."

"Let him go, Sister," Juanita said, her voice quivering as though she were about to give way to tears.

"Fine. Hurry."

Noah turned and carefully made his way off the trail. LaNora watched intently, saying a silent prayer that no harm would come to the groundskeeper and that Dominica would be all right. As he drew nearer, LaNora could hear him talking to Dominica. She was not answering or moving. He crouched down beside her and put out his hand and turned her over, onto her back. His head bowed and he put his hand to his brow.

"What is it, Mr. Talbot?" Victoria said.

Noah looked over his shoulder. "I'm sorry, Sisters. She's dead."

"Dead!" Juanita shrieked.

"Stay where you are!" he ordered in a deep, resounding voice that echoed off the trees. Juanita froze. "There could be more traps. I'll bring her to you."

Noah carefully lifted the lifeless body of Dominica. She looked so small in his arms even though she was nearly five and a half feet tall. When her head dropped back, LaNora could see that Dominica's white wimple and cheeks were mottled with something dark. As he drew nearer, she could see hints of red. *Blood.* She made the Sign of the Cross and covered her mouth.

"Dear Mother of God," Victoria gasped when she saw Dominica's face.

Juanita trembled and wept, her hands reaching out to touch Dominica but hovered inches from her.

"We'll take her back to the lodge," Victoria said with a cold, unemotional tone.

"Lead the way, Sister," Noah said.

The trip back to the lodge was quiet and slow. Noah laid Dominica down gently on the sofa in the sitting room. It was then that LaNora was able to get a look at her.

"What happened?"

"It appears that whoever set the trap came back and let her out."

"But—" LaNora looked at Dominica's ankle.

Dominica's right foot hung limply over the edge of the sofa, obviously broken. She cringed and looked back at Noah.

"For whatever reason, from the look of the ground and her clothes, she must have tried to get away from her would-be rescuer. She dragged herself off the trail into the woods. At some point she was struck in the back of the head," Noah explained.

"But why?" Juanita sobbed.

"We don't know," Victoria answered.

The sound of the front door opening caused everyone to turn and look toward the foyer.

"It's snowing!" Grace announced in a loud, excited voice as she stepped into view.

Victoria rushed at the young novice and grabbed her by the arm. "Where have you been?" she demanded, pulling Grace into the sitting room.

"You're hurting me!" Grace said defiantly and pulled against Victoria's grasp.

"You could be a lot more than hurt, Sister! Now, sit down," Victoria said, shoving Grace into one of the empty chairs in front of the sofa.

Grace's jaw dropped and her mouth gaped open when she saw Dominica's body lying on the couch. "What's going on?" she asked and looked at the Victoria.

"We have been out looking for you all morning and afternoon. Where were you?" Victoria said.

Grace looked at each of them and then back at Victoria. "I was out looking over the property like we're supposed to."

"Where specifically?" Victoria said.

LaNora glanced at Noah who had slipped away to stoke the embers in the fireplace back to life. He placed a couple of logs on them and flames began to lick the bark as if in anticipation of consuming them.

"I asked you a question," Victoria said.

LaNora looked at Grace. She watched as Grace

tightened her jaw.

"You're not Mother Abbess," she said. "I don't have to answer you."

"As the senior member of those here, I am your superior and you will answer me," Victoria said.

"And if I don't?"

Victoria looked at the others. "Sister LaNora, Sister Juanita, will you escort Sister Grace to her room with me."

"Yes, Sister," they answered.

Grace's brown eyes widened when she saw the two nuns approaching. LaNora felt her anger take over and she grabbed Grace by the arm and pulled her to her feet. Grace winced in pain and drew back her free arm to strike LaNora. Juanita grabbed it and twisted it behind her.

"Stop it!" Grace screamed.

"Answer my question."

"No!"

"Let's go," Victoria said.

They made their way into the foyer and up the stairs with Victoria leading the way. LaNora could hear keys rattle and knew what was coming.

When the four reached Grace's room, Grace began to pull against them again.

"Why are you doing this? What's going on?" she shrieked.

"Put her into her room," Victoria said. "As long as she won't answer my questions, I won't answer hers."

Juanita released her hold once LaNora and Grace had entered the room. Grace pulled free of LaNora's grasp and lunged at the door.

"Oh, no you don't!" Juanita said and blocked Grace's path. She pushed her back into the room and moved away so LaNora could shut the door. Victoria stepped forward and locked the door from the outside.

"Do you think that will hold her?" LaNora asked.

"It should. That's one thing that is nice about these old

doors, they're solid wood. I doubt she knows how to pick a lock," Victoria said and tucked the key ring back into her pocket.

When they reached the stairs, Victoria stopped and turned to face them. "Sister Juanita, would you please get a couple of sheets from the linen closet and bring them to the sitting room?"

"Yes, Sister."

The sound of Grace hitting the door caused Victoria's lips to purse in an angry expression. Without a word, she walked back to Grace's door.

"Your time would be better spent in silent reflection and prayer, Sister," she said through the door.

"Let me out!" Grace screamed.

"Silent prayer, Sister," Victoria said and returned to the stairs.

"How long are we going to keep her locked up?" LaNora asked while the descended to the first floor.

"That depends on her," Victoria answered. "We can't have her running off with someone out there intent on killing us."

"Killing us?" Juanita said and gasped. Her eyes were wide with confusion and fear.

"Let's take care of Sister Dominica and then we should talk," Victoria said. She took one of the bedsheets from Juanita.

LaNora looked into the sitting room and saw that Noah was not there. A thud outside caught her attention and she excused herself before going to have a look.

Noah had just put the last piece of firewood onto the neatly stacked pile against the wall beside the front door when LaNora stepped outside.

"I thought I should get another load of wood before it gets too dark out and the snow begins to pile up," he said.

"Are you sure you'll be okay?"

Noah looked at her and smiled. "I don't know what's

going on but, yes, I think I can manage."

"Don't be too long," LaNora said, stepping closer to him. "We should talk."

"Don't worry. I won't be."

"Remember, you're staying here with us until we can find a way to get out of here. So, you might want to bring a few things from your cabin."

"I will. Now, you best get back inside."

LaNora turned and walked back to the front door. She hesitated and looked over her shoulder just as Noah took the handles of the wheelbarrow and started for his cabin.

"And where were you?" Victoria said when LaNora walked into the sitting room.

"I, um—Mr. Talbot has gone for more firewood," she said.

"Fine. We can't leave Sister Dominica in here, it's too warm. Please give me a hand and let's put her in the office. I think it will be cold enough. Sister Juanita, will you get the door?"

LaNora and Victoria gently picked up the body swaddled in the bedsheets. LaNora was thankful they had covered Dominica's face. It made moving her feel more like carrying a heavy sack of potatoes and less like carrying the dead body of her friend.

Juanita opened the door to the office that was down the hall to the right of the stairs. An oxblood leather sofa sat against the wall just inside and faced a large desk. The window behind it looked out over the backyard. To the left of the sofa, a bookcase covered the entire height and length of the wall. In the corner, behind the desk, opposite the hall door, stood a gun cabinet with several rifles aimed at the ceiling.

"Sister, let's put her on the couch," Victoria said, her voice tired and strained.

They gently laid the body down and then stepped back. Making the Sign of the Cross, they all knelt down. Victoria led them in a short prayer.

Moments later, the three met back in the sitting room and warmed themselves by the fire. There came a knock on the front door and before anyone could answer, the door began to open.

"Sisters, it's me, Noah."

"Oh, Mr. Talbot, you startled us," Victoria said.

"I'm sorry."

"Please, join us in the sitting room, there's something I wish to say and I want you to hear it, too."

"Okay." He followed her into the sitting room and dropped his duffle bag by the door.

Sister Juanita stood between the end of the sofa and the fireplace. Sister LaNora sat in a chair facing the sofa.

"Please, have a seat, Mr. Talbot," Victoria said and motioned toward the sofa. After he sat down, she continued. "I want to apologize to you for the scene a few minutes ago. I shouldn't have let my temper get the better of me."

"It's quite all—"

Victoria held up her hand to stop him. "It's just that we can't have Sister Grace running off like she has been, not with someone out there who is trying to kill us."

"Kill us?" Juanita asked. "Who is trying to kill us? Why?"

"I wish I knew," Victoria said.

Looking out the window at the darkening sky Noah stood up. "Excuse me, but I should get one more load of firewood before the snow starts to pile up."

"Of course, Mr. Talbot," Victoria said, excusing him.

The three watched him leave before LaNora spoke up.

"It's getting late and I should be getting dinner. Sister LaNora would you give me a hand?" Victoria said.

"Certainly."

"Sister Juanita, will you keep an eye on the fire for us until Mr. Talbot returns?" Victoria asked.

"Yes, Sister," she answered and picked up the poker.

In the kitchen, LaNora kept stealing a glance out the

window at the path. A light above the shed door came on, illuminating the ground where the snow had begun to stick. LaNora whispered to herself, "Please keep him safe."

"What was that, Sister?" Victoria asked when she stepped up to the sink to rinse off a head of lettuce.

"Oh, I was just saying a little prayer for Mr. Talbot," she said.

"I see. Well, just be careful," Victoria said and shook the water from the lettuce. "Can you slice up a cucumber for me?"

"Yes, Sister," LaNora answered.

LaNora had just finished setting the table when Noah walked into the foyer. He hung his coat on an empty hook beside the door.

"Brrrrr," he growled and shook his head and arms.

"Just in time, Mr. Talbot," Victoria said in greeting when she walked into the dining room.

"The snow is starting to come down pretty good out there," he said. "I finished stacking the firewood outside for us. We should be able to keep warm for several days, now."

"Splendid. Come, have something to eat. It's been a long day."

"That it has," Noah said and followed Juanita into the dining room.

The four sat two on either side of the table. They bowed their heads while Victoria offered prayer.

"What about Sister Grace?" Noah asked and looked at the three.

"She will eat in her room. I'll take a tray to her after we're finished," Victoria answered.

"Sister, is there a connection with the six of you, other than you are nuns from the same order?" Noah asked while he dropped a spoonful of mashed potatoes onto his plate.

Juanita choked on her water.

"That reminds me," LaNora said looking across the table at Juanita. "The other day, when you told Sister Abigail that you didn't understand why Sister Grace had to come, it wasn't about her being a novice, was it?"

Juanita looked at Victoria and LaNora. "No," she said.

"I knew it!" LaNora said triumphantly. "It's because the rest of us were part of the same novitiate class, am I right?"

"Yes."

Noah looked confused.

"Mr. Talbot, Sisters Dominica, Juanita, LaNora, and I entered the convent at the same time. Sister Abigail was our Novice Mistress, she was in charge of us. Sister Grace entered our convent a little over a year ago," Victoria answered.

"Oh, I see," Noah said. "So the four of you—"

"Actually, there were five of us," Victoria interrupted, "but one didn't make it."

"Didn't make it? Did she leave?"

"No, she passed away," LaNora answered.

"Died?" Noah nearly shouted.

"Well, actually, she committed suicide. We don't like to talk about it," Victoria said.

"I don't blame you, but who was she?" Noah continued to prod while he helped himself to the green salad.

"Her name was Sister Rhonda but we called her Ronnie," Juanita answered.

"She came to the convent as Rhonda Jacobson. If she would have made it to vows, it would have changed," Victoria said.

"Changed? Oh, now I'm confused," Noah said and shook his head.

"She was a troubled soul," Juanita said.

"In what way?" Noah asked.

"She was under a lot of pressure from her family who wanted her to become a nun."

"Sister Juanita, we don't know that for certain," Victoria said.

"But that's what she told me, Sister."

"Still, we shouldn't talk about this."

"Why not?" LaNora asked. "It's been nearly ten years. We can't just bury our feelings. Ronnie was a sweet girl who didn't deserve to die so young."

"That may be true, but talking about it now is not going to change anything."

"No, but it might help us to understand why we didn't see it coming. I mean, why didn't any of us try to stop her?"

"I never thought she was serious," Victoria said. "How many times did she moan and say she was going to kill herself if she failed a test or she'd rather die than be anything but a nun?"

"We could have told Sister Abigail," LaNora said.

"That would have resulted in her expulsion. You know how tough Sister Abigail was on her."

"We could have told Mother Claire," Juanita said.

"But we didn't. We were new ourselves and working hard to adjust to a new way of life. We didn't know," Victoria said.

"I just wish. . ." Juanita began to cry.

"This is why we shouldn't talk about this," Victoria said. "Sister, it's okay. It wasn't your fault or any of ours."

"My head knows that," Juanita said, wiping her tears away with her napkin, "But my heart is harder to convince."

"True," Victoria agreed.

There was a bit of silence while the four continued to eat their meal. LaNora tried not to look across the table at Noah for fear Victoria would catch her and try to make it more than it was, but she could not help herself. She watched his mouth while he chewed. His lips pressed together and the muscles in his jaw tightened as he ate. There was even a moment when he looked at her and their eyes met. She quickly looked at Victoria to calm the rising butterflies in her stomach. When they were finished eating, Noah excused himself to check on the fire in the sitting room.

"Sisters, let's get these dishes cleaned and put away," Victoria said. She stacked the plates and took them into the kitchen. LaNora and Juanita gathered the empty salad bowls, platters, and glasses and followed her.

"When is Mr. Hastings due to return?" Juanita asked.

Victoria turned around, her mouth agape and her eyes wide. "With everything that's happened I completely forgot," she said.

"Forgot what?" Juanita asked.

Victoria looked at LaNora and took a deep breath. "I'm afraid he isn't coming back, Sister."

Juanita gave her a confused look. "And you know this because?"

"We found the van," LaNora said. "It crashed in the woods just short of the main road."

"What about Mr. Hastings?"

"We couldn't find him," Victoria said. "There was a lot of blood on the driver's seat and floor. The windshield was smashed."

"Where could he have gone?"

"Mr. Talbot thinks he couldn't have gone anywhere on his own," Victoria said.

A thud from upstairs reminded LaNora that they needed to take a tray of food to Grace. She grabbed a tray from the cupboard and fixed a plate of a hamburger patty, mashed potatoes, green beans, and salad. She wrapped a fork in a napkin and stuck it in the pocket of her habit.

"I'll take Sister Grace her dinner," she said after pouring a glass of milk and setting it on the tray.

"Splendid," Victoria said. "You'll need this." She held out her key ring.

"I'll go with you," Juanita said. She wiped her hands on a dishtowel and grabbed the keys. "We won't be long," she said over her shoulder to Victoria.

CHAPTER EIGHT

The lodge was quiet. Juanita was in the sitting room reading her Bible by the warm fire. Victoria was in the kitchen making cinnamon rolls and dinner rolls for the next day. Grace was still locked in her room and giving everyone the silent treatment. She even refused her dinner tray which LaNora reluctantly took back to the kitchen.

"I don't know if we're doing right by keeping her locked in her room," she said to Victoria while she emptied the plate into the small compost pail.

"With everything that has happened and her insolent behavior, we have no choice. It's for her own good," Victoria said without looking up from kneading the dough.

"I know, but. . ." LaNora left the kitchen without finishing her thought.

She walked back to the foyer and looked into the sitting room.

"Where's Mr. Talbot?" she asked, interrupting Juanita's reading.

"He said something about getting some fresh air," Juanita answered and turned the page.

LaNora grabbed her cape from the hook and flung it around her shoulders. Quietly she opened the front door and slipped out. The night air was cold. A layer of snow had already blanketed the gravel driveway and the surrounding grounds. In the glow from the porch light, she could see large flakes of snow still coming down.

She looked up and then down the covered porch. At the corner of the lodge, she spotted the tall silhouette of the groundskeeper. The butterflies awoke and fluttered. She pressed her palm over her stomach to calm them. Slowly she strolled past the sitting room windows to the corner where Noah stood.

"Sister Juanita said I would find you here," she said.

Noah jumped and turned around sharply, his hands clenched into fists.

"Oh, my," LaNora said. "I didn't mean to startle you."

Noah's broad shoulders relaxed and his hands returned to their normal ease. "It's okay. What are you doing out here?"

"I could ask you the same thing."

"Thinking," he said. "I can't believe this is happening and I don't understand why to nuns of all people."

"I wish I knew. I had an uneasy feeling about this when I saw Mr. Drummond. There was something about him that didn't look right. He didn't look comfortable in a suit and tie, and he kept referring to the papers as if it were some script."

"Perhaps it was. I mean, he's not the owner's attorney. So, could he have been some sort of actor?"

"That's what I tried to tell Sister Victoria but she thought I was confusing him with someone else," LaNora said. She turned to look out at the clearing across the driveway. "What I don't understand is why would whoever is doing this not give us a reason? I mean if we did something to them and this is their revenge, I could understand but to not tell us why doesn't make any sense."

"Yeah, it doesn't," Noah said. "I've been thinking

about that girl who offed herself, that Rhonda Jacobson. The name sounded familiar to me. I dated a girl in my freshman year in high school once who had that name. We didn't connect, in fact, instead of a goodnight kiss she slapped me."

"Why? What did you do?"

"Nothing. I think she was a little mental. One minute she was clingy and the next she was mad about something or another."

"What happened to her?"

"Well, we never went out again. But being the sort of guy I was back then, I lied to my buddies and said she was an easy lay. It spread like wildfire in the locker room and throughout the school. She left mid-year and I heard her family moved away."

"That is awful," LaNora said.

"I know," Noah said, sounding apologetic. "It's one of the many regrets I have."

"You aren't alone in that department. I have some of my own," LaNora said. "Where did you go to school?"

"Roosevelt in Portland. Why? You don't think it's the same girl do you?"

"I don't know. It's just too coincidental that they had the same name," LaNora said. "So, how long do you think it will snow?"

"Hard to tell. It hasn't shown any signs of letting up. In fact, just the opposite. It's coming down a lot harder since I've been out here."

LaNora stared out at the snow-covered ground and felt trapped. With snow covering the ground there would be no way of spotting a trap like the one that Dominica stepped in. They could not walk out of there even if they wanted to.

"May I ask you a personal question," Noah said and leaned his back against the post so he could face LaNora.

"You may, but as long as I can decide if I should answer it."

"Fair enough," Noah said with a smile. "What

possessed you to become a nun."

LaNora smiled back. "I wouldn't call it possession exactly, quite the opposite. I know that other girls imagine their wedding day or a fabulous career but ever since I was a young girl I dreamed of becoming a nun."

"Why? I mean, didn't you want to fall in love?"

"Oh, I did. There was one boy, Luke. He was the school's star quarterback and all-around athlete. We were an item all through high school. I really did love him, a lot."

"So, what happened?"

"The desire and pull to become a nun were stronger."

"Wow. When I was a kid, I wanted to be a fireman like my dad. But that all changed when he and my mom divorced."

"Was it his idea?" LaNora asked.

"No, it was my mom's. She was tired of his work schedule and all the overtime he put in. She was mad at him but took it out on me. She was also a drunk."

"I'm sorry."

"It's all water under the bridge. After that, I didn't think past the moment. But out here," he said and looked at the falling snow, "here I have a lot of time to think. Sometimes too much. It would be nice to have someone to share my life with. I'm just afraid that what I did after prison would scare women away."

"Then they don't deserve you."

"You're very kind."

"And so are you. Don't kid yourself."

"I know what I am. Life has a way of giving you a reality check. Spending time in jail, now that was like learning how to swim by being thrown into the deep end of the pool. A real eye-opener to how adult life wasn't going to be a walk in the park."

"You can't compare being in jail with what everyday life is like for the majority of the population."

"No, but it can really cause you to reevaluate what you

really want, what's important."

"You're a strong, handsome man, Noah. There are bound to be thousands of young women out there who would love to get to know you and love you for the man you are, not the past you."

"But I'm not so sure I want to know them anymore. I mean, I may have found someone."

LaNora looked at him with shock mixed with surprise. "Really?"

"Yes," he said. "The two of us haven't known each other very long but given the right opportunity that could change."

"That's wonderful," LaNora said and then shivered. Pulling her cape closed she started to turn back toward the door but Noah stopped her, his hands firmly grasping her arms. Her eyes widened. Their eyes met. Her pulse quickened. He leaned in, she did not pull away or try to stop him. Their mouths opened to each other. His hands released her and she wrapped her arms around him. For a moment, she was eighteen again, in the parking lot at senior prom with her date. She did not care who saw them. Suddenly, a vision of Sister Victoria watching her with judgmental eyes popped into her head. Instantly she pulled away and covered her mouth, her eyes fixed on Noah.

"No," she said. Turning away she hurried back inside.

"How was it out there?" Sister Juanita called from the sitting room.

LaNora did not answer. She rushed up the stairs to her room and closed the door behind her. *Oh dear God, what have I done?* She grabbed her Bible from her bedside table and opened it but closed it just as quickly. Turning around she began to pace. *Why did I let him kiss me? Why didn't I push him away and leave? I took a vow.*

A knock on the door halted LaNora.

"Sister, is everything okay?" Victoria said through the door.

"Yes, Sister," LaNora answered.

"Are you sure? Might I talk with you for a moment?"

Noah. Did he say something to her? There's no way he would tell her. Would he?

LaNora took a deep breath and tried to calm herself. Closing her eyes for a moment and exhaling, she felt her heartbeat return to normal.

"Yes," she said and opened the door.

Victoria motioned for LaNora to come out of her room. LaNora put her Bible on her bed and joined Victoria in the hall.

"I've been thinking about our wandering sister. Perhaps I was a bit hasty locking her in her room."

"What choice did you have?" LaNora said while they made their way toward the stairs.

"I think I should let her out and all of us sit down and have a talk, try to impress upon her the importance of not wandering off."

"As you wish, but I'm not convinced it will do any good."

LaNora followed Victoria to Grace's door.

"Sister, I'm unlocking your door," Victoria called out and inserted the key. "You may come out."

There was no answer.

"Sister Grace, I know you are upset about this but we need to have a talk. Please come out."

Still silence.

Victoria looked at LaNora with questioning concern in her eyes. "Grace, I'm coming in," she said through the door. She gave the doorknob a turn and pushed the door open.

The light was on inside the bedroom. The bed sat against the right wall with a small square table beside the headboard. A dresser stood against the left wall and an armoire to the right of the door. Across the room, the curtains billowed as the cold night air filled the room.

"Oh no she didn't!" Victoria said and rushed to the

window. LaNora followed her.

"I don't believe it," LaNora said.

"Come, we must let Sister Juanita know."

"We aren't going to try to find her now are we? It's dark out and snowing."

"No, we will have to wait," Victoria said while she shut and locked the window.

Juanita was still in the sitting room on the sofa but her Bible was on the table beside her. LaNora froze when she saw Noah stoking the fire and adding another log to it. Slowly she walked into the room keeping her eyes on him.

Noah glanced over his shoulder and gave her an apologetic smile before turning back to the fire.

"It appears that our wandering nun has flown the coop again," Victoria said.

"What?" Juanita nearly shouted and stood up. "How?"

"Through the window."

"You've got to be joking. It's freezing outside and her cape is in the foyer."

"I know but she's gone."

"Well, I'll get my cape," Juanita said and started to leave.

"No," Victoria said and stopped her. "We're not going to risk anyone else getting hurt over her."

"But she could—"

"I know, but we've tried all we can to curb her in. Sometimes we have to learn things the hard way," Victoria said.

"I could look for her," Noah said standing up and facing the three.

"That's very kind of you, but no. Sister Grace won't stay out there long. She'll come back on her own."

Noah nodded then walked across the room to a chair in a dim corner of the room and sat down. LaNora watched him out of the corner of her eye.

"I think the best thing for us to do is wait here,"

Victoria repeated. "Give me a hand. I want to do a little rearranging if that is okay?" She turned to Noah.

"Sure, be my guest," he said and stood up to give her a hand.

Together they slid the sofa around until it faced the fireplace and its back was to the French doors to the foyer. While LaNora turned the coffee table parallel to the sofa, Juanita dragged a chair over to where the sofa had been. Noah grabbed the other chair and moved it next to the hearth. Once they were finished, the three sat down on the sofa and let Noah have his pick of the chairs.

LaNora stared at the flames, letting her thoughts wander back to the kiss on the porch, that magical moment when she felt beautiful, like a woman again. It was at that instant she realized and admitted to herself that she wanted him to kiss her. Since the first time she saw him, she wanted to feel what it was like to have his strong arms holding her, to feel his heart beating against hers, and to feel desirable again. It was wrong, she knew that too. She had dedicated her life and made a vow to God. She belonged to him. The feeling of guilt was overwhelming. Like Eve she had fallen for the bait and crossed the line. *Oh, God, will you ever forgive me?*

"Sister," Victoria repeated and touched LaNora's arm startling her out of her thoughts. "You're trembling, what is it?"

"Nothing," LaNora said and shook her head. "Just thinking about everything that's happened. How are we going to get out of here?"

"I don't know."

"There has to be a way. We can't just stay here like caged animals waiting to be the next one."

"We will be all right," Victoria said firmly.

"I'm sorry," LaNora said.

"Nonsense, we are all thinking the same thing. Maybe in the morning, the snow will have let up and we can see our way clearer."

"Yes, Sister, everything will be better in the daylight," Juanita said.

"I hope so." LaNora settled back in the corner of the sofa. She yawned and closed her eyes.

CHAPTER NINE

LaNora woke with a start. She looked around the room and for a moment could not remember where she was. Gradually the fog of sleep lifted and she realized she was in the sitting room. The fire had burned down to embers in the fireplace but the room still seemed bright. She looked at the window and realized it was morning. Standing up she felt something fall to the floor. It was a blanket. She yawned and stretched then readjusted her veil and habit before picking up the blanket and draping it over the arm of the sofa where she had been sleeping.

The sound of Noah's deep voice from within the lodge awakened the dread and guilt from the night before and brought her into the foyer.

"Well, good morning, Sister," Juanita greeted as she descended the stairs.

"Good morning, why didn't you wake me before you went to bed?"

Juanita gave a little laugh. "We all slept downstairs. Must have been the warmth of the fire. You drifted off right away. I think Mr. Talbot was next. We heard him snoring a little in the corner."

"Did Sister Grace return?"

Juanita frowned and shook her head.

"Figures. I don't understand why she gets away with this. When we were novices we would have been disciplined severely and if that didn't work, asked to leave," LaNora said, sounding thoroughly disgusted. She glanced at the front door and then looked back at Juanita. "Is it still snowing?"

"It seems to have let up. Mr. Talbot thinks sometime shortly after he came inside last night because it's only three inches deep in the open. Come with me, I need some coffee."

LaNora took a deep breath and inhaled the scent of freshly brewed coffee. *Coffee would be good right about now.* She followed Juanita to the kitchen.

"Well, good morning, Sisters," Noah greeted and stood up from his seat at the island.

"Good morning, Mr. Talbot," Juanita answered alone.

LaNora avoided eye contact with him and looked at Victoria instead.

Victoria glanced at LaNora and smiled. "How did you sleep?"

"I'll have to get back to you on that," she replied and tilted her head from side to side to loosen the tense muscles in her neck.

"Well, breakfast is ready so let's go into the dining room."

Everyone grabbed either a platter, cups, and pitcher or plates and flatware and headed into the next room. Juanita passed out the plates and let everyone arrange their own place settings. Victoria returned to the kitchen and brought back the carafe of freshly brewed coffee.

After saying a prayer, the four began to eat their meal.

"Sister, may I ask a question?" Noah asked.

Victoria looked across the table at him. "Certainly, what's on your mind?"

"Are we not allowed to talk during breakfast?"

Victoria laughed. "I'm sorry, Mr. Talbot, old habit. We usually eat our meals in silence at the Abbey, but we may speak here if you wish."

"I was thinking about Sister Grace," Noah said. "I'm wondering if we should go looking for her now that it has stopped snowing."

"I don't think we should risk it. I mean, we have no idea where she went. Plus there's the possibility of more traps waiting for us out there."

"I agree with you, Sister," Victoria said, looking at Juanita. "Sister LaNora, you are awfully quiet this morning. Is everything all right?"

LaNora stopped midchew and turned toward Victoria seated beside her. She nodded while she finished swallowing. "I agree with Sister Juanita. We shouldn't risk injury or worse to try to find her. Sister Grace is an adult and as an adult, we all have to deal with the consequences of our own actions." She looked at Noah as though speaking about herself as well.

"That's a bit harsh, isn't it, Sister?" he said and sipped his coffee.

"I was once told that life is a series of choices. We are told in the Bible that whatever we sow, we shall reap. So, harsh or not, we all have to learn to make better choices."

"Look at you, Sister," Juanita said with a slight chuckle. "Getting all philosophical so early in the morning."

LaNora suddenly felt self-conscious and ducked her head while she continued to eat.

"Well, I can take a look around while I go for more firewood. Looking at the sky out there, I think I should bring back a good supply in case it begins snowing again."

"That would be kind of you but, please, don't go out

of your way. We don't want you getting hurt," Victoria said.

"I'll be careful," Noah assured her.

"I have been racking my head," Juanita said, "trying to figure out why someone would be doing this and why us?"

"And have you come up with anything?" Victoria said.

"It has to be something tied to our novitiate year. I think it must be about Ronnie," Juanita said. "I mean, our old Novice Mistress and all of us reunited. It has to be."

"But what's the connection with Sister Grace?" LaNora asked.

Juanita frowned. "I don't know."

"It could be something else. Someone who dislikes our Abbey or a certain sister. . ." Victoria said and looked at LaNora.

"I don't think it's her anymore," LaNora said and looked at Noah, "Because Mr. Talbot might have a connection."

"What?" Victoria said, looking across the table at the groundskeeper.

"It might be another coincidence but," Noah said and gave LaNora a look that said he was not pleased to be forced to share more of his personal life with everyone. He took a deep breath and continued. "When I was a freshman in high school, I knew a girl named Rhonda Jacobson. Her family moved before the end of the school year. But I don't know if it's the same person as your Ronnie."

"That is a coincidence," Victoria said.

"Do you have a yearbook from that year?" Juanita asked.

"After I settled in here, my mother sent me a box of my old things. I never looked in it. I just shoved it under my bed. I'll pull it out when I go for more firewood and check. I have to warn you, though, even if I do, I don't know if Rhonda is going to be in it. As I said, she left before the end of the year."

"We understand and appreciate your willingness to even try," Victoria said.

After the meal concluded, Victoria asked LaNora to assist her in the kitchen with the cleanup. Instantly LaNora felt worried and a bit nauseous. *Did Noah tell her about the kiss? Would he?* LaNora picked up the dishes and flatware and followed Victoria into the kitchen. She placed the dishes beside the sink and went to retrieve the rest from the dining room. To her relief, Juanita had already left, leaving Noah alone.

"Did you say anything about last night to Sister Victoria?" LaNora whispered while she gathered the platters and cups.

"Tell her what?" Noah.

"Will you keep your voice down," LaNora asked, glancing over her shoulder at the kitchen door. "You know what I'm talking about."

"The kiss?" Noah whispered.

LaNora nodded.

"That was our special moment," he said, smiling as if he was still savoring the memory. "No, I didn't tell her."

"Good. It can never happen again. I'm a nun."

"You're still a woman."

"I dedicated myself to God. I'm not free to get emotionally involved with a man."

"Oh, is that what was happening?" Noah smiled.

"No!" LaNora snapped back, sounding exasperated. "It can never happen again, is that clear?"

"If you say so."

"I do." LaNora leaned against the kitchen door and pushed it open. She backed into the kitchen and let the door close between them. "Here are the last of the dishes," she announced and placed them beside the sink.

Victoria turned the faucet off and placed the stack of plates into the soapy water. She let them begin to soak while she readjusted the faucet over the right side of the sink and turned on the water on to just a dribble. She felt the water to make sure it was hot.

"I have a question, Sister. How did you find out about Mr. Talbot and Ronnie?" Victoria asked while she ran a dishrag over a platter.

"He told me last night while we were out on the front porch watching the snow falling," LaNora said while tying the apron's strings behind her back.

"I see."

"I know what you are going to say and before you do, be assured it will never happen again."

Victoria shut the water off. "I wasn't going to say a word. After all, we all have to bear the consequences of our actions. Isn't that what you said?"

"Yes, Sister," LaNora answered like one of her pupils after being given a scolding.

"Then we will not speak of it again. Here," Victoria said and handed the clean wet platter to LaNora. "You can dry."

"Happily," LaNora said.

With her duties in the kitchen finished, LaNora retreated to her bedroom for a bit of solitude. The lodge was quiet once again. Noah had gone for more wood and hopefully his yearbook. Juanita was tending the fire in the sitting room and Victoria had begun making a pie for the night's dessert.

She was about to enter her room when the sound of footsteps directly over her head caused her to duck. She looked down the hall at the door. *So that's where you are!* She headed for the door while still hearing someone stirring overhead. She grabbed the doorknob and tried to turn it. *Locked.* Angered at the thought of Grace being defiant, she tried harder to turn the doorknob to force it open. It was no use. Remembering the doorknob was glass, she decided not to try to force it again for fear of getting cut. "How did you get up there?" she said out loud. Too frustrated and angry to be alone, she headed back down the stairs to the kitchen.

"I think I know where Grace is," she announced letting the door swing shut behind her.

Victoria looked up, setting the half-peeled apple down along with the paring knife. She wiped her hands on the small towel on the island. "Where?"

"The attic. I was about to enter my room when I heard someone walking above me."

"Let's go see."

LaNora led Victoria up the stairs to the hallway. They stood and listened. Silence. Victoria looked at LaNora and was about to speak when there was a loud thud above them. They both ducked.

"See, I told you," LaNora whispered. "I tried the door at the end of the hall but it's locked. There has to be some other way to get up there."

"I haven't seen anything," Victoria said. "Perhaps Mr. Talbot knows of something? We'll ask him when he returns."

Victoria headed back to her baking in the kitchen. LaNora followed, still seething inside over not being able to open the door. She pulled a stool out from under the edge of the island and positioned it so she could see through the window above the sink. Confident she had a clear view of the path that led to his cabin she sat down.

"I'm surprised you can remain so calm," she said, watching Victoria peel the last of the apples.

"Calm? Who said I'm calm? I'm going out of my mind trying to figure out why this is happening and how we can get out of here," Victoria said while she sliced the apple, letting the pieces fall into the waiting pie shell. "I find by baking I can think clearer. My mother was the same way. She would bake whenever she felt stressed. I'd come home from school some days to fresh baked bread, cookies, pies, cakes. I knew not to be loud or ask any questions. To this day I never knew what made her so stressed."

"Didn't you ever ask her? I mean when she wasn't stressed."

"Once, when I was very young but she just smiled and said it was nothing." Victoria put the knife down and picked up the measuring cup of cinnamon mixed with sugar. She sprinkled it over the top of the apples before adding a few dobs of butter. Picking up the rolling pin with the top crust wrapped around it, she sealed the pie.

"That reminds me," LaNora said. "With everything that has happened, I completely forgot about Thanksgiving. What day is it?"

"Tuesday."

"Are you still planning on celebrating?"

Victoria looked at her. "Of course. Just because all of this is going on doesn't mean we shouldn't pause to give thanks for all the good things we've received. Besides, I just told you, baking helps me focus."

A movement outside caught LaNora's eye. In the distance, she could see Noah returning with a wheelbarrow loaded with more firewood.

"He's back," she announced.

Victoria closed the oven door and looked through the window in the outside kitchen door. "I hope he was able to find his yearbook."

"Let's go find out."

The snow had begun to fall again by the time the three sisters and groundskeeper finished stacking the load of firewood outside the front door.

"We should be more than fine now," Noah said while following the others inside.

"Thank you again, Mr. Talbot. We really appreciate your help," Victoria said. She hung her cape on the wall hook between the sitting room and the front door.

"Did you see any sign of Sister Grace?" Juanita asked. It was clear by her tone that she was becoming worried for the young novice.

"Not even a footprint in the snow," Noah said. "I'm sorry."

"It's all right," she answered. "You tried."

He removed his coat and that's when LaNora saw the large book stuck under the waistband of his jeans. She looked away quickly fearing she would blush.

"You remembered," Victoria said.

"Yes, I did. I even took a moment to check for her picture. She's in here. Let's go sit by the fire and I'll show you."

LaNora moved the two chairs closer to the coffee table. Victoria sat on the sofa beside Noah while LaNora and Juanita took the chairs. Noah placed his yearbook on the coffee table and opened it. He scanned the page and then flipped several pages toward the back of the book. He stopped and pressed the book flat.

"She's right there," he said pointing to a tiny black and white portrait of a young, dark-haired girl.

Victoria sat forward and eyed the picture. She had a puzzled expression. "I'm not sure," she said.

Noah turned the book around so Juanita and LaNora could have a look.

"That's her!" Juanita said confidently. "I would know her at any age."

LaNora agreed. The girl did resemble a younger version of the Ronnie she knew. She looked at Noah with wide-eyed shock.

"This means your being here was no coincidence," she said. "If this is about Ronnie, then you are as much a target as we are."

Noah looked at the picture of the young girl and made a dismissive snort. He closed the book and stood up. He started to leave but stopped in the doorway to the foyer. Turning his head he said, "I need some air." The sound of the front door shutting behind him seemed to echo throughout the lodge.

LaNora looked at the other two. "Do you think this has something to do with Ronnie?"

"I think we're grasping at straws," Victoria said and stood up. She pulled the small kitchen timer from the pocket in her habit and looked at it. "I need to check on the pie."

LaNora watched her leave. "Am I the only one who thinks that we've been called here for some act of revenge?"

Juanita remained silent. She stared at the fire.

"What's the matter?" LaNora asked, seeing the dampness in Juanita's eyes.

"I was just remembering that night," she answered, still staring at the fire. "Ronnie and I were on our way to Vespers and Sister Abigail stopped us. She said she wanted to see Ronnie right after prayer and then entered the chapel. Ronnie was so worried. I could see her hands trembling during the psalmody.

"After we were dismissed, I went with Ronnie to Sister Abigail's office. I waited outside while she went in. I could hear Sister Abigail's voice but couldn't quite make out what she was saying. But Ronnie must have been closer to the door because I could hear her crying. She was begging and pleading for another chance. Then I heard Sister Abigail's voice clearly, 'Face it, you're not cut out to be a nun.' Ronnie nearly shouted that she couldn't go home, she'd rather die than face them."

"What did Sister Abigail say to that?" LaNora asked.

Juanita looked at her. "She said, 'That's your choice.'"

LaNora's mouth gaped in surprise. "I can't believe her. I mean, I knew she was mean and strict but I never thought she would be cold and cruel. You should have reported her to Mother Abbess."

"And tell her I was eavesdropping?" Juanita said. "No. Besides, the thought never occurred to me at the time."

The room fell silent except for the crackling of the burning logs. LaNora sat back in her chair and became lost in a memory. Ronnie's cubicle in the novice dorm was beside hers. Separated by a curtain, she had heard Ronnie weeping into her pillow. She had wanted to say something to her, to console her but she feared the wrath of Sister Abigail more. After all, being out of your bed after lights out was strictly forbidden unless you needed to use the privy. It would be grounds for punishment or expulsion. And being caught speaking during grand silence was just as bad. LaNora had turned over and pulled her pillow over her ears.

"Her eyes were open," Juanita said.

"What?" LaNora said and the memory vanished.

"When I found her. Her eyes were open. I checked for her pulse, but there was none. So, I closed her eyes."

"Juanita, I had no idea."

"I woke up in the middle of the night and needed to use the bathroom. I heard water spilling over. When I went into the bathroom, that's when I saw her. She was sitting on the floor with her back to the wall. Her arms were by her side. There were blood and water all over the floor. She had stopped up the sink and turned the hot water on. I turned it off."

"Juanita—"

"I heard her crying that night after lights out. I thought about going to her, consoling her, telling her we could go to Mother Superior in the morning, that Sister Abigail didn't have the final word, but I did nothing. I let her cry."

"It wasn't your fault."

Juanita looked away from the fire. "I wish I could be so sure."

"Juanita, I heard her too. I think all of us did that night. If we would have gone to her and Sister Abigail caught us, we would have been in trouble ourselves."

"I know. I think that's why I didn't." Juanita wiped the tears from her cheeks. "Do you really think what's happening now has anything to do with Ronnie?"

"I don't know but I also don't believe in coincidences either," LaNora said. "Come on, let's go see what Sister Victoria's up to in the kitchen."

They both stood up and at the same moment heard the front door open. They walked into the foyer.

"Look who I found," Noah said, closing the front door.

"Sister Grace, where have you been?" Juanita said and rushed to the shivering novice.

LaNora grabbed a cape from the hook and draped it over Grace's shoulders. "Come, let's get you warmed up by the fire. Were you outside all night?"

Grace did not answer. She shivered and pulled the heavy, black wool cape tighter around her neck. She did not resist Juanita's guiding her into the sitting room and toward the warmth of the fireplace.

"You shouldn't have climbed out the window," Juanita said. "Sister Victoria was just worried about you. Sister Dominica is dead."

Grace's eyes widened in shock and she looked at Juanita and then LaNora. "Oh, no. How? Why? What happened?"

"When you wandered off, we all went looking for you," LaNora said with a tinge of anger beneath her words. "Sister Dominica stepped in an animal trap. When we found her, she had been struck in the head and was dead."

"So, you can't go wandering off like this. It's not safe," Juanita said in a gentler tone.

"But Mother said we were to survey the property for the Abbey."

"No, that was all a ruse," LaNora said. "The owner of this property is not dead. He didn't will us this land. We were brought here for some. . . other reason."

Grace looked at them and then back at the fire.

"So, no more running off," Juanita said with her arm around Grace's shoulders. "We don't want to lose you, too."

Grace nodded.

LaNora turned around and saw Noah standing in the doorway watching them. She walked around the sofa to him and they both moved into the foyer.

"Where did you find her?" she asked.

"She was huddled down between a tree and the hot tub in the back. Her white habit blended in with the snow. If she hadn't looked up, I would never have seen her."

Glancing over her shoulder at Grace and Juanita, she said. "Well, thank you for finding her." She looked into his eyes and put her hand to his whiskered cheek.

He grabbed her arm and pulled her toward the front doors. Before she could stop him, he wrapped his arms around her and kissed her. She gave into him and reveled in the moment.

The sound of the kitchen door opening sent a flood of panic washing over LaNora like a cold shower. She pushed away from Noah and wiped her mouth. Glancing at him she saw him smile.

"No," she whispered.

"What's all the commotion?" Victoria said when she saw the two in the foyer.

"Mr. Talbot found Sister Grace," LaNora answered.

"Splendid," she said and led the way into the sitting room.

CHAPTER TEN

"I can't believe tomorrow is Thanksgiving," LaNora said while she poured the coffee grounds into the filter and carefully placed it onto the stem of the coffee urn. "At the Abbey, there's always a feeling of excitement. Here, with everything that has happened. . ."

"We still have a lot to be thankful for, Sister," Victoria said. She cracked another egg and emptied it onto the griddle.

"I know, but it just doesn't seem right to be joyful when Sister Abigail and Sister Dominica are lying dead in the other room. How are we going to get out of here?" LaNora asked, sounding exasperated.

"I had contemplated us all walking out but now with a foot of snow on the ground. . ."

"But the nearest town is over twenty miles away," LaNora said.

"True, but we would have only needed to make it to the main road, I'm sure someone would have stopped to help us." Victoria shook her head and cracked another the egg. "But now I don't think anyone would be traveling in this weather."

"So now what?"

"We wait. Didn't Mr. Talbot say that he was expecting a delivery in a week?"

"Yes, but in this weather, who knows if he'll be able to make it," LaNora said.

"I guess we can talk about this later. Do you mind going upstairs and letting Sister Grace and Sister Juanita know breakfast is about ready?"

"Yes, Sister, I'll be right back." LaNora took off her apron and hung it with the others by the back door before heading upstairs.

She headed straight for Sister Juanita's room and knocked lightly on the door. "Sister Juanita, breakfast is almost ready," she said into the door.

The door opened and Sister Juanita stepped out into the hallway. "Sorry, I must have overslept."

"That's quite all right. It was an emotional day yesterday."

They stopped at Grace's door and before either could knock, the door opened.

"Good morning," Grace greeted them with a cheery smile.

"I trust you slept well," LaNora said.

"Oh, yes. I think I'm finally getting feeling back in my feet and hands."

"That's good to hear."

The three headed for the stairs but a loud thud above them caused them to stop.

"What was that?" Juanita asked.

"That's enough!" LaNora said. She rushed down the hall toward the last door on the right with Juanita and Grace running after her.

"Sister, what are you doing?" Grace asked.

LaNora grabbed the doorknob and tried to turn it. It did not move. She yanked on the door a couple of times and then began to hit the door with her palm.

"Who's up there?" she demanded.

There was no response.

Again she beat her hand against the door and yelled. "We know someone is there, come out."

Again, nothing.

"Stop it!" Grace shouted.

"We need to get in there," LaNora said, turning away from the door.

"Why?" Grace asked.

"Because I'm tired of whoever is up there toying with us like a game of cat and mouse."

"The owner doesn't want us to go up there. So we should ignore it."

LaNora looked at Grace. "And how do you know this?"

"Because. . ." she looked at Juanita and then back at LaNora, "because we don't have a key."

"Fine," LaNora said and brushed past them and headed for the stairs. She was still seething inside over the noise in the attic but now she was becoming suspicious of the novice in their midst.

Moments later the three entered the kitchen. Victoria was putting the last pancake on the platter and looked up.

"Good morning," Victoria said when LaNora entered the kitchen. Victoria put the last pancake on top of the others on a large platter and turned off the griddle. "What was all that commotion upstairs about?"

The kitchen door opened and Grace entered followed closely by Juanita.

"We heard someone in the attic," LaNora answered.

"Where's Mr. Talbot?" Juanita asked.

"He went to check on his cabin," Victoria answered. "He should be back any minute." She glanced over her shoulder at the window above the sink. Turning back around she picked up a stack of plates and handed it to Grace. "Let's go ahead and set the table."

"Yes, Sister," Grace said and left the room.

"Take this tray and help her, please," LaNora said, scooting a tray of glasses, silverware, and napkins across the island to Juanita.

"Okay," Juanita said with a bit of hesitation. She picked up the tray and left the room.

Once the two were alone, LaNora pulled Victoria toward the corner by the backdoor.

"What's this about?" Victoria asked.

"How much do we know about Sister Grace?"

"I don't know anything. Sister Juanita would know more. Why?"

"Because just now, upstairs, she said the owner doesn't want us to go up in the attic. And she knows that we weren't given a key for that door."

"She must have deduced it from our earlier conversations."

"She wasn't here whenever we talked about the attic," LaNora said. "She was gone."

Victoria looked away while she thought. "Oh my, you're right."

"So, what do we do?"

"Nothing right now. We'll just have to keep an eye on her. Grab a couple of those platters. I'll get the orange juice and syrup."

They had no sooner finished setting the table when the front door opened and Noah walked into the foyer. The legs of his denim jeans were wet from his knees down and snow clung to his heavy boots. He shivered and stomped his feet and made a growling noise as he shook off the cold.

"Oh, I didn't mean to keep you waiting," he said when

he noticed the four sisters all watching him from the dining room.

"You didn't. You're just in time," Victoria said. "Come, join us."

Noah quickly hung his coat on an empty hook and stood behind his chair at the table. They all bowed their heads and Victoria said the prayer.

"It smells delicious," Noah said while he pulled out his chair and sat down.

"How does it look out there?" Sister Grace asked.

"White. Very white," Noah said with a grin. He looked across the table at LaNora who did not appear amused. "Actually, it's not bad. Thank goodness for the trees along the path back to my cabin, the snow isn't very deep at all. It's only in the open areas that it's about a foot deep. Deeper in some of the drifts."

"Do you think it will stop your delivery guy from coming?" Victoria asked while she passed the plater of sliced ham.

"Nah," Noah grunted and shook his head. "Joe's used to this stuff. He was born and raised here so this is nothing to him, besides, this could all be gone by next Friday."

"Really?" Juanita said, sounding hopeful.

"Yes," Noah said and nodded. "We've had it snow all day and by the next morning, it was gone. But on the other side of the coin, one year it snowed and was on the ground for four months. We had nearly three feet then."

"Oh no," Juanita said and groaned. "Let's hope it goes away fast."

"Not to change the subject," LaNora said. "But when we were upstairs, we heard something in the attic again. It sounded like something heavy hit the ceiling—floor, above us. Do you know if there is another way into the attic?"

"I'm afraid not," Noah said.

"There has to be a way up there because I keep hearing someone moving about," LaNora said.

"Really?" Noah said. "How odd."

"I think we should just forget about it," Grace said.

"Why is that?" Victoria asked.

"Because the door's locked," Grace said. She looked at them and appeared to be nervous.

"Well, from what we know, it was the owner's deceased daughter's room."

Grace choked and grabbed her water glass, taking a quick drink. "I'm sorry," she said, "please, continue, Sister Victoria."

Victoria kept her eyes fixed on Grace. "I can understand why he wouldn't want anyone up there."

"But someone is," LaNora said. "And I think we should find out who is up there."

"I agree," Sister Juanita said. "It could be the person who killed Sister Abigail and Sister Dominica."

"I disagree. If it is, what would stop him from killing us, too?" Grace said.

Victoria's head tilted as she looked at the young novice. LaNora glanced at Victoria and read her expression. She caught it as well.

"What we need is someone who can pick a lock," LaNora said.

"I can," Juanita said.

Everyone stopped eating and looked at her.

"How do you know how to do that?" Victoria asked.

Juanita looked at their faces. "Oh, it's nothing bad. I had to pick a lock on the toolbox once. I locked the key inside by mistake. Rather than having to saw the lock off, I tried to pick it and it worked."

"Well, after breakfast would you mind giving it a try?" LaNora asked.

"No," Grace said before Juanita could answer.

"Yes, Sister, I will give it a try," Juanita said, ignoring the novice's protest.

"I can't be a part of this!" Grace shrieked and jumped up from her seat. She started for the foyer.

"Sister Grace, get back here!" Victoria said and stood up.

Grace continued into the foyer.

"I'll get her," Noah said and jumped up. He rushed into the foyer but Grace was already out the front door. He followed but moments later returned without her. "I'm sorry, she disappeared."

"How is that possible?" LaNora asked. "There's snow out there. She must have left tracks."

Noah shrugged and shook his head. "I don't know. I didn't see any."

"Well, she couldn't have vanished into thin air," LaNora said and then her eyes widened. "Are we sure she even left the lodge?"

"Enough speculation. Let's finish our meal and then have a look at the attic," Victoria said and sat back down.

They finished their breakfast in silence. Afterward, the three sisters cleared the table. Victoria left the dishes to soak while they met in front of the door to the attic.

"Now, if you are able to get the door open," Victoria said to Juanita, "we will let Mr. Talbot go up first. We don't know what or who is up there. Is that okay with you, Mr. Talbot?"

"Yes," Noah answered.

After trying the doorknob one more time to be sure it was still locked, Juanita knelt down in front of the door. She took out two thin metal picks that were bent at right angles on one end from her pocket. Seeing the surprised looks on the others' faces she smiled.

"They were left over from assembling the doorknob on the garage back home."

She inserted one end of the tool into the keyhole and then the end of the second tool. She gently moved the top pick while holding the bottom one still.

"I think it's working," she said and continued wiggling the pick.

There was a soft click sound and then Juanita sat back on her heels. She withdrew the tools and reached for a hand to help her back to her feet. Noah obliged.

"There, it's unlocked," she announced and turned the knob.

The door hid a staircase that rose steeply to the upper floor. The stairwell was narrow, only the width of the door. The bare wooden boards of the steps were well worn from years of use.

LaNora kept close to Noah to ensure she would be the second to see what was at the top. Her heart began to beat faster when she stepped on the first riser. In the dim light that shone from above, she could see the wall was stained where a handrail should have been.

Noah stopped once he could see the upper floor. "You've got to be kidding me."

"What? What is it?" LaNora asked.

He did not answer but instead continued to the top. LaNora quickly followed. Her mouth gapped in surprise at the sight of a child's bedroom. A bed with a white canopy sat in the center of the room against the far wall, directly over the hallway downstairs. In the walls to the right and left of the bed were gables with windows that looked out over the front and back of the lodge. Lace curtains hung in front of them, defusing the daylight. To the left of the bed was a rocking horse. From the size of it, it was meant for a young child possibly first to third grade. A dresser sat against the wall to the right of the bed, its top just inches below the start of the slanted ceiling. A framed picture, a music box with a tiny horse on its hind hooves, a silver brush and mirror, and a small box sat on top of the dresser covered in a layer of dust. On the floor at the foot of the bed lay an old oval braided rug, its color muted by dust. Opposite the stair landing sat an adult-size wooden rocking chair. LaNora stared at it and slowly walked over to it. A chill came over her when she realized that unlike everything else in the room, there was no dust on the chair.

"What a lovely room!" Juanita said from behind LaNora.

"She must have been well-loved," Victoria said.

"It's as if they left it as some sort of shrine," LaNora said. Her eyebrows pinched together while she looked at the size of the room and remembered the loud noises. She looked at the stairs and then at the wall at the head of the bed. She backed up to the stairs and then paced across the room to the wall behind the headboard.

"That's odd," She said, turning around and looking back at the stairs again.

"What? What's odd?" Noah asked, still standing at the top of the stairs with his arms crossed and his shoulders a bit slumped as if he were uncomfortable being there.

"The room is too small," LaNora answered.

"Too small? When I was a kid I would have killed for a room this big," he answered and then realized what he had said. "Sorry, figuratively speaking about the killing. I really wouldn't have killed. . ."

LaNora looked at her sisters who were trying not to laugh. "It's okay, I understand," she said letting him off the hook. "No, the room doesn't extend far enough to where I heard the noises." She turned back toward the wall and started feeling the surface. "They came from the other side of this wall. There has to be a way to get over there."

"What are you doing?" Victoria asked.

"Looking for a door or something."

"I don't see a door," Juanita said while she watched LaNora feel the wall.

"There has to be," LaNora said.

"Perhaps there's another entrance somewhere else? We should go," Victoria said.

LaNora turned away from the wall. She started to leave but noticed the corner of a piece of paper peeking out from beneath the pillow on the bed. Carefully she pulled it out. Her eyes widened and her mouth gaped open. She looked at the stairs and saw that everyone had already gone. Tucking the photo beneath her scapular, she quickly hurried to catch up.

When she reached the second floor, the others were already halfway to the stairs. She closed the door and picked up her pace. She reached them as they began to descend the stairs.

"When I was a young girl in Mexico," Juanita asked, "I had a cousin who drowned. My tia was devastated. She set up a little shrine in the corner of her dining room with his ashes, pictures, and an old shirt he used to wear. She would light candles and say prayers for her son. I wonder if that is why the owner left the room untouched?"

"So, are you through snooping around," Grace said, her tone a sounding a bit angry. She stood in the center of the foyer with her arms folded over her chest.

"We weren't snooping," Victoria said. "We were looking for clues to who is behind what happened to Sister Abigail and Sister Dominica."

"And did you find anything?" Her tone remained bitter and angry.

"No," Victoria said.

"It's such a lovely room," Juanita said. "You should have seen it."

"I don't need to," Grace said sharply, "it was locked for a reason and I think it was unchristian for you to violate the owner's privacy."

LaNora did not say a word. She stared at the young novice and tried to figure out why she was getting so worked up.

"Well, we won't be going back up there," Victoria said. "So, no harm, no foul. Is that all right with you?" She looked at Grace who eventually nodded.

"I think I'll go to my room and do some reading and meditating," she said.

"I'll call you when the noon meal is ready," Victoria said.

LaNora watched Grace ascend the staircase before she turned to Victoria. "I'll give you a hand."

"Splendid."

"I'll check the fire," Noah said.

"Do you think it would be all right if I stepped outside for a moment, get some fresh air? I won't leave the front porch. In fact, I'll stay by the door," Juanita asked.

"I suppose," Victoria said, "but, be careful and stay alert."

"I will," Juanita said. She reached for her cape but it was not on the hook. "Has anyone seen my cape?"

"Oh," LaNora said as she remembered. "I think we borrowed it for Sister Grace last night."

Juanita looked at the ceiling and then back at the others hanging on the wall. "I'll just borrow hers, then." She wrapped the white, floor-length, hooded cape over her shoulders and raised the hood, completely covering her black habit. "I'll be right outside the door."

In the kitchen, Victoria set out a large metal bowl and gathered the ingredients for making her abbey-famous meatloaf.

"Grab five large potatoes, please," Victoria said while she tied her apron around her waist.

LaNora hesitated a moment.

"What?" Victoria asked.

Standing at the end of the island, LaNora looked back at the hall door and pulled the photograph from beneath her habit. She set it on the island in front of Victoria.

"I found this under the pillow on the bed," she whispered.

As Victoria looked at the photograph her eyes widened in shock. "How did this get here?"

"I don't know," LaNora answered. "I remember when this was taken. It was Easter Sunday and a week before Ronnie died. The reporter from the Catholic Sentinel wanted a picture of the novices for the article she was writing."

"I remember," Victoria said. "The article was pulled before the Sentinel came out because of Ronnie's death. The reporter gave us each a copy of the photo but Sister Abigail wouldn't let us have them. Vanity, she called it."

"Maybe the reporter gave this to Ronnie's parents?"

"So, you think this is Ronnie's family's home?"

"It seems to fit, don't you think?"

"I don't know. Maybe it was someone from the Sentinel? I'm so confused. Let's get cooking."

LaNora gathered several potatoes into the fold of her apron and brought them to the island where she emptied them out, catching them before they had a chance to roll off the edge.

"Do you think five will be enough?" she asked Victoria.

Victoria looked across the island at the size of the potatoes and smiled. "I think that is sufficient but maybe you should grab another."

"Sure. You know, you would think that as hard as Mr.

Talbot works he would eat more."

Victoria watched LaNora grab another potato from the bushel basket behind the door to the hall. "Are you doing okay?" she asked when LaNora returned to her stool at the island.

"Yes. I'm fine. Why do you ask?"

"Oh, I noticed you've stopped calling him by his given name," Victoria said. "So, are you past your crisis?"

LaNora did not look at Victoria while she spread a paper placemat in front of her and picked up the peeler. "Yes, I think I am," she said and began peeling a potato.

"That's wonderful to hear. I will admit, I was worried for you."

"Well, you needn't have been," LaNora said and watched as Victoria reshaped the mound of ground beef, bread crumbs, onion, and spices into six miniature loaves and placed them onto a large broiler pan.

"I know but it's my job as your big sister," Victoria said with a grin.

"We're the same age. Well, you are a few months older but still. . ."

They both laughed.

After rinsing and cutting the potatoes in half, LaNora gently dropped them into a large pot of water and set it on the stove. Turning back to the island, she said, "What do you think about Sister Grace's reaction to the room in the attic?"

"What's there to think?" Victoria said while she searched the cupboard of canned vegetables.

"I just find it strange that she was so upset about out wanting to see what was up there."

"Who knows what goes on in her head."

"That's true," LaNora said. "But I just can't help feeling that she is somehow connected to what's going on here."

"Feeling?" Victoria said, sounding a bit skeptical.

"Hey, I was right about that Mr. Drummond not being an attorney."

"True. But why would someone want to harm us after all these years and over something which we had nothing to do with?"

"Are you so sure?" LaNora said. "I mean, I heard Ronnie crying that night. I could have comforted her but instead, I ignored her."

"She would have done what she did anyway. Once a person gets that thought into their head, if they can't shake it off themselves, then nothing anyone can do will prevent it. Delay it, maybe, but not prevent it. That's my opinion, mind you. I'm no psychiatrist and that's what she needed."

"I suppose," LaNora said. "I just wish there were some way to find out who the owner is. Then at least we would know what we are up against."

"Possibly."

"It would be a start, at least."

"Well, let's think about it later. Right now, we need to finish preparing the—" Victoria turned around and noticed the sink full of the breakfast dishes. "Oh no. I completely forgot," she said and rolled up her sleeve. "Grab a fresh towel and dry for me, please."

"Sure," LaNora said.

That night after everyone had gone to bed, LaNora found she could not sleep. She had made sure the door and window of her room were locked, but still when she closed her eyes, sleep evaded her. Finally, giving up, she decided to go downstairs and try her mother's old remedy of warm milk and honey. She put her robe on over her floor-length nightgown and tied the sash about her waist. Running her hand over her hair, she pulled her long braid over her shoulder.

The hallway was dimly lit by a nightlight at the top of the stairs. She looked up and down the corridor before venturing out of her room. At the top of the stairs, she looked over the banister. Flickering light from the fire in the sitting room illuminated the foyer. There was no sign of anyone so she proceeded.

Before heading to the kitchen, she decided to check the front door. As she crossed the foyer, she glanced through the open doors of the sitting room, secretly hoping to glimpse Noah sleeping. He was not there. She quickly checked the lock on the front door. It was secure. Turning around she let out a gasp and quickly covered her mouth.

"I didn't mean to startle you," Noah said, standing in front of her with only a pair of pajama bottoms on and a steaming mug in his hands.

LaNora quickly looked away. "Noah—I mean, Mr. Talbot, I didn't know you were up."

"I couldn't sleep so I went to the kitchen for some warm milk. What about you?" he asked.

LaNora looked at the mug in his large hands. Gradually she raised her eyes to see his face. He was staring at her. She coyly looked away and fumbled with her braided hair. "Same," she said. "Only, I put a bit of honey in it. It sort of sweetens it and helps me relax."

"Humm. I guess I'll have to try that," Noah said. "Mind if I join you?"

LaNora could feel her pulse quicken and nervousness spread through her. "If you like."

She slipped past him and headed to the kitchen. Walking straight to the refrigerator she took out the pitcher of milk. After rinsing the pan Noah had left in the sink, she poured some milk into it, enough for them both. Noah had gone to the cupboard. He took out the jar of honey and set it on the island.

"Thank you," she said and put two teaspoonfuls into the pan and stirred it in. She placed the pan on the stove and turned the burner to low.

Noah followed her and stood beside her.

"You have lovely hair," he said. "It's a shame to hide it under that veil."

LaNora nearly dropped the spoon in the milk. Her stomach fluttered. She swallowed hard and took a deep breath.

"I hope you don't mind my saying that," Noah said and stepped closer.

Out of the corner of her eyes, she could see his tight stomach and broad chest covered with dark hair. The thought of what it would feel like to touch it, to run her hand over it tempted LaNora. She closed her eyes and felt her strength drain from her arms and legs. She said a silent prayer and continued stirring the milk.

"It's ready," she said and carefully she carried the pan over to the island. She filled both cups and then rinsed the pan and left it in the sink.

Noah sat down on a stool across from LaNora.

"So, Mr. Talbot, why couldn't you sleep?" she asked and took a sip of her warm milk.

"I don't know. I keep thinking about that room in the attic and something about it sounded familiar. I haven't seen it before, I know that. But there's something. . . What about you?"

"I keep thinking about something I found when we were up there."

"Found? What?"

"A photograph of our novitiate class. It was taken a week before Ronnie died."

"Oh," Noah said. His brow furrowed. "That sort of narrows it down, don't you think? I mean, this must have something to do with Ronnie and her family."

"If only there was a way to find out who the owner of this lodge is. Then we would know for certain."

"Doesn't the picture sort of tell us?"

"No, it could belong to whoever is behind it and it may have nothing to do with the owner."

"I see. But the bedroom, isn't that telling?"

"I don't know. I can't think," LaNora said.

"Have you had a look around the office?"

"Not personally, why?"

"Maybe there's letterhead or a piece of mail or something that could tell you."

"Let's have a look."

Before Noah could say another word, LaNora rushed past him and through the swinging door to the hallway. She reached the office door first and grabbed the doorknob and gave it a turn. Her shoulders slumped. "I forgot. It's locked," she said.

"I have a key," Noah said and handed her his mug. "Wait here." He rushed into the sitting room and a moment later LaNora heard the jangling of keys. "Here we go," he said.

LaNora stepped aside and let the groundskeeper unlock the door.

"Thank you."

Noah opened the door and turned on the light. The sight of Dominica's swaddled body lying on the sofa momentarily took LaNora's breath away. She'd forgotten they had placed her in there.

LaNora turned her attention to the large desk. She went behind it and pulled on the drawer handle but it did not open.

"I don't suppose you have a key for the desk?" she asked.

"No, but I might know how to open it." He walked around to the back of the desk. LaNora moved aside. He knelt down and reached under the center drawer. "I had an uncle once who used to hide the key to his desk. . ." He stretched his arm further beneath the drawer until he could feel the back. He worked his fingers along the back and then suddenly stopped. A grin spread across his lips. "Bingo!" he said triumphantly and pulled the key free from its hiding place. He unlocked the desk and stood up. "It's all yours," he said and playfully bowed to LaNora and presented the desk to her.

She stepped forward and opened the center drawer.

"Empty?" she said sounding both shocked and surprised. She shut it and tried another and another. "Nothing," she said with a bit of annoyance in her tone. "I can't believe someone would lock an empty desk. What am I missing here?"

Noah shrugged his shoulders and shook his head.

LaNora glanced at the bookcases filled with books. "Ah-ha!" she said leaving the desk and crossing the room to the bookcase. "I wonder if there is something in one of these? Maybe an author signed a book for the owner?"

"That's an idea," Noah said. "I'll start down here and you start at the other end. Check the books but put them back in their place."

LaNora moved to the end of the bookcase by the window and began to pull the books out, one at a time, and opening them to their title page. After she checked the bottom shelf, she moved up to the next. "Anything?" she asked.

"Nothing yet," Noah replied.

By the time LaNora reached the top shelf she had developed a rhythm, book, page, shelf, book, page shelf, book—it would not budge. "That's odd," she said and stood on tiptoes to get a better grip on the book. With her left hand, she held onto a lower shelf to steady herself. With her right hand, she pulled harder and then heard a click and felt the bookcase move away.

"Oh my Lord!" she gasped and caught herself before

she fell into the bookcase.

"Wha—" Noah started to ask but stopped when he saw LaNora push the bookcase inward.

"A secret passageway," LaNora said, staring at the spiral staircase that went down to the cellar and up toward the second floor. "This is so cliché."

"This is too crazy," Noah said. "I had no idea there was a secret passage in this place."

"I wonder where it goes?" LaNora asked.

"There's only one way to find out," Noah said. "Shall I go first?"

"By all means," LaNora said.

Noah stepped in front of her and felt the wall for a light switch. "I knew you had to be here," he said and flipped the switch. A light from somewhere above came on and illuminated the stairwell with a dim glow. "Let's see where this goes," he said and started up the staircase. LaNora quickly followed him.

The circular staircase made two turns and then they reached a landing on the second floor. LaNora noticed a door but did not make any attempt to open it.

"Sister Grace's room is on the other side of that door," she whispered. "She didn't go out the window at all. She is mixed up in this somehow. I knew it!"

"Come on, let's see what's up there," Noah said, pointing toward the attic.

Another two revolutions and they had reached the top of the staircase. The light bulb that hung at the end of a wire in the stairwell cast its light into the attic causing the many trunks, boxes, and wooden barrels to throw long shadows on the floor. Something across the room caught LaNora's attention. Forgetting she had one more step before she was on the attic floor she tripped. Noah caught her and lifted her to her feet. Her hands felt his chest and her pulse quickened. She looked up into his eyes and before she could think, she opened her mouth to his. Slowly she slipped her arms under his and around his back. Their mouths parted and she felt his rough cheek against hers.

"You are so beautiful," he whispered into her ear.

The light caught the gold band on her left hand. She felt a jolt deep inside her chest and pushed away.

"No, no!" she said and ran the back of her hand over her mouth. "I'm a nun. I can't do this."

"But—" Noah started to protest but stopped. "I'm sorry. It was my fault."

"Look, over there," LaNora said, changing the subject and willing the guilt she felt to disappear.

"What? I don't see anything."

"In the corner, the cot."

Noah saw it. Together they made their way around the pile of boxes. A cot was set up right above the hallway below. A small lamp that matched the one in Victoria's room sat on a small stool beside the cot. The lampshade was dented as if it had fallen and hit the floor.

"Dear Lord, someone is camped out up here," she said.

"We better get out of here," Noah said.

"Not until I have searched this area for any clues," LaNora said and picked up the pillow, lifted the blanket and then knelt down and to look under the cot.

"Anything?" Noah asked, looking over his shoulder at the darkness behind him.

"Nothing. Let's go."

Moments later the two were back on the first floor standing at the foot of the main staircase.

"What are we going to do?" LaNora said.

"I don't know. Should we wake the others and tell them?"

"No! Sister Victoria will ask why I was alone with you

again. No. I'll have to figure out a better way to let them know."

"Fine, I'll let you tell them when you're ready. You better get back to your room. Make sure you lock your door."

"I will," LaNora said and looked at him again. She felt the urge to give him a kiss goodnight but turned away and headed back up the stairs.

CHAPTER ELEVEN

It was six in the morning when LaNora, dressed in her habit, came down the stairs. She nearly tripped when the front door opened but caught herself.

"Good morning, Sister," Noah said after glancing at her. "The snow is coming down again." He tried closing the door behind him but his arms were loaded with several logs for the fire.

"I'll get that," LaNora said and quickly closed and locked the door. Noah had already disappeared into the sitting room when she turned around. She closed her eyes and took a deep breath. She hated the feeling of guilt that now lived deep in her chest. She pushed away from the door and headed to the kitchen where she knew she would find Victoria.

"Good morning," Victoria said without looking up from rolling out the dough for fresh cinnamon rolls. "Sleep well?"

"No," LaNora admitted. "I don't think I will ever sleep again, at least not until we get back to the Abbey."

"I know," Victoria agreed. "I heard you pacing in your room last night. Did you hear the noises coming from the attic?"

"No."

"It sounded like someone was walking around up there. I think I even heard voices."

"Really?" The guilty feeling in LaNora's chest began to expand and mix with fear. "Could you hear what was said?"

"No. I could only hear a man's voice but I couldn't make out what he was saying. He was definitely talking to someone, though. I'm surprised you didn't hear it, you were in your room."

"I was?" LaNora said.

"Yes, as I said, I heard you pacing."

The knot in her chest loosened. LaNora felt herself relax. She went to get her apron. "I must have been deep in prayer. I didn't hear a thing."

"Well, now we know whoever it is isn't alone. So we need to be very careful," Victoria said. She rolled the cinnamon, sugar, and raisin covered dough into a log. Taking a knife from the drawer, she sliced it into round discs and placed them in a greased pan. "Once I have these in the oven, I thought the four of us could meet in the sitting room for our Morning Prayers."

"Sounds good."

"Is everything okay? You seem a bit quiet this morning."

"I'm just tired and a bit anxious. I really want to get out of here."

"We will. I have a plan," Victoria said. "For now, please let the others know about Morning Prayers."

LaNora removed her apron and left it on a stool by the island. She hurried out of the kitchen, letting the door swing until it stopped by itself. When she reached the foyer, Sisters Juanita and Grace were on the landing.

"We'll be holding Morning Prayers in the sitting room

shortly," she said while she passed them on her way back to her bedroom.

Alone in her room again she leaned against the closed door. "Get a grip on yourself," she whispered sternly to herself. "What is the matter with you?" The voice in her head took over. *It was only a kiss, well three kisses, but you kiss your father when you see him.* "Yes, but I don't kiss him like that," she answered aloud. *It's no big deal. It's not like you're in love with him, are you?* "Enough!"

LaNora thrust her hands into her pockets and started to pace. She stopped when her right hand felt something in her pocket. She pulled it out. It was a crumpled piece of paper. She unwadded it. It was the note from her pupil. She tore it into confetti and dropped it into the wastebasket beside the dresser. Grabbing her Bible from the nightstand, she headed back downstairs.

After Morning Prayers, LaNora returned to the kitchen with Victoria to help prepare breakfast for everyone. The service had been just what LaNora needed to assuage her guilt. She felt more like herself again.

The kitchen smelled delicious with the scent of freshly baked cinnamon rolls and hot coffee. When Victoria brought the turkey out of the walk-in refrigerator, LaNora remembered that it was Thanksgiving.

"I'll get the bird ready if you will handle breakfast this morning," Victoria said and placed the turkey on the counter beside the sink.

"Sure," LaNora said. She tied her apron strings into a bow behind her back. Grabbing a few potatoes from the basket she began peeling them to make hash browns. "We'll have scrambled eggs, sausage links, hash browns, toast and cinnamon rolls. What do you think?" she asked Victoria.

"Sounds perfect," Victoria answered a bit distracted. She was preparing the dressing to stuff in the turkey.

LaNora did not notice. She took the bowl of grated potatoes over to the stove and dumped them onto the hot griddle. She glanced at the pot of boiling water on the stove. "Your pot is boiling, Sister," she said and over her shoulder at Victoria.

Victoria stood at the sink looking out the window.

"Is something out there?" LaNora asked.

"I thought I saw something moving by the shed," Victoria answered. "Mr. Talbot is still inside, isn't he?"

"Last I knew he was in the sitting room with Sister Juanita and Sister Grace," LaNora said and looked through the window in the door. "It's probably just the snow falling off a tree branch or something."

"Suppose you're right. I do wish it would stop snowing."

Juanita, Grace, and Noah walked into the kitchen right when LaNora spooned the last of the scrambled eggs onto a platter.

"Perfect timing," LaNora said. "Would you two mind setting the table for us?"

"Not at all," Juanita answered.

Victoria watched the young novice pick up the tray of plates, glasses, napkins and silverware and head into the dining room. She walked over to Juanita. "I want to thank you for staying close to Sister Grace. Please, keep an eye on her and don't let her run off."

"Oh, I'm not letting her out of my sight. I don't trust her but she's not going to disappear on my watch."

LaNora smiled and handed Juanita the platters of potatoes and sausage.

Victoria finished stuffing the turkey and placed it into the oven. "It should be ready about three, just in time for early supper."

After saying a prayer, Victoria began passing the

platters around the table.

"I can't believe it's Thanksgiving and snowing," Juanita said. "I don't think I've ever seen snow this early."

"We've even had it as early as the middle of October," Noah said.

"Oh dear, that's just not right," Victoria said. "What do children do on Halloween?"

"People out here don't trick-or-treat on Halloween. There aren't that many families and everyone lives too far apart for that."

"Do you think the snow will let up soon?" Victoria asked.

"Unfortunately there's no way of knowing," he said and glanced across the table at LaNora.

LaNora kept her head down but she could feel him watching her. She said a silent prayer to keep her nerves in check.

"So, what do you Sisters normally do on holidays?" Noah asked.

"Oh, we usually spend the mornings in prayer and meditation. Then we gather for Mass at eleven," Juanita said.

"Afterward, we have our noon meal. Then the afternoon is spent by us teachers getting ready for classes to resume," Victoria said. "What do you do?"

"Well, nothing really. By this time of year, it's usually just me here. Sometimes I'll chop wood or go for a ride on the quad to make sure the fences are holding up and that none of the deer have caught themselves on it."

"Does that really happen?" Juanita asked.

"I'm afraid so. The fawns try jumping the fence like the does and every once in awhile, get a leg caught. They thrash around until they either free themselves or die from exhaustion."

"Oh my, the poor things," Juanita said, her voice

sounding as though she were about to cry. "Isn't there something you can do?"

"If I catch them in time but usually I'm too late. It really is rare," Noah said in an attempt to reassure her. "One year while I was out along the northern fence line, the neighbor saw me and invited me to have dinner with him and his family. That was special."

"I thought the neighbors were gone this time of year," Victoria said.

"They are, normally. That year was the exception. Since Mr. Blair retired a couple of years ago, they are here for a few weeks and then gone. I think they use their cabin as a vacation spot or for hunting."

"How—"

The lights in the dining room went out, interrupting LaNora. Only the dim daylight that came through the windows kept them from being in total darkness.

"It must be the generator," Noah said. "I'll take a look."

"No, you stay and finish your breakfast. Sister Grace and I will check it out," Juanita said while she stood up. "Come, Sister Grace."

"Are you sure? I know these machines."

"I'm sure I can figure it out. I've worked on a generator or two," Juanita said. "It will be fine. Especially with the two of us."

"Sister Victoria," Noah said, turning to the head of the table.

"It's fine. We can keep an eye on them from the kitchen. If they need help, they can signal us," Victoria said and pushed her chair back from the table.

LaNora put her napkin on the table and stood up.

From the kitchen window, the three watched as Sister Juanita and Sister Grace trudged through the near knee-deep snow. With Grace in her white cape, it was hard to see her against the snow.

"Good, they've reached the shed," Victoria announced. "It shouldn't be too much longer now."

LaNora looked at the lights hanging over the island anticipating them coming back on. Nothing.

"She's a stubborn one, isn't she," Noah said while he looked out the window.

"I'm sorry?" Victoria said and looked at him.

"Sister Juanita."

"Yes, Mr. Talbot, she can be insistent at times," Victoria said with a bit of a laugh.

The lights above the island came on.

"Ah, they've fixed it," Victoria said.

"See, Mr. Talbot, Sister Juanita can be handy, too," LaNora said. "Shall we finish our meal?"

"I'll check the oven and be right there," Victoria said.

LaNora and Noah started back to the dining room. As she reached for the door, there was a loud boom outside and the lights went out.

"What was that?" LaNora yelled.

"It sounded close," Noah said and rushed to the window. Victoria and LaNora were quick to follow. "Oh my God!"

A thick cloud of black smoke billowed through the open door of the shed. Inside, flames appeared to cover the floor. Juanita stumbled out into the clearing and collapsed face down in the snow.

Forgoing their capes and coat, the three rushed outside.

"Juanita!" Victoria screamed. She ran as best she could through the deep snow, ignoring the biting cold on her legs. "Juanita!" she screamed again.

Juanita did not answer and did not move. She lay still,

her hands buried in the snow.

Noah rushed past Victoria, heading straight to the shed. He grabbed the extinguisher that was just inside and to the left of the door and pulled the pin. Foam sprayed from the nozzle and doused the flames.

Victoria fell to her knees beside Juanita and gently turned her over onto her back. Her face was blackened with oily soot.

"Careful of her hands," LaNora said, noticing that they were burned.

"Juanita," Victoria said in a calmer tone. "Juanita, wake up."

Juanita's eyelids fluttered. She coughed and gasped for air. Her eyes opened and she looked at Victoria and then LaNora.

"S-s-she tried to kill me," she said in a raspy tone.

"Who?"

"Sister Grace," Juanita said and coughed.

Victoria gave LaNora a look that said you were right before turning her attention back to Juanita. "Let's get you inside. Are you able to stand?"

"I think so," she answered. With Victoria holding one of her arms and LaNora the other, they helped Juanita to her feet.

"Where is Sister Grace?" Victoria asked.

Juanita turned her head toward the shed but did not answer.

"Go, see to her. I'll help Sister Juanita back to the lodge," Victoria told LaNora.

LaNora released her hold on Juanita's arm and following the path Noah made in the snow to the shed. "Mr. Talbot?" she called.

Noah emerged from the back of the shed, sooty sweat streaking his face and smelling of smoke. "Don't come in here," he said.

"Is Sister Grace—" LaNora did not finish her question. She already knew the answer from the look in his eyes.

"I'm afraid she's dead," he said, confirming it.

"What about the generator? Is that what exploded?"

"No, it was a gas can. The fire damaged the main generator beyond repair. It's dead. The other generator is pretty much undamaged and working but it's smaller and was only for backup."

"Does that mean we won't have power?"

"I'm afraid it will be reduced to minimal. Things like the refrigerator and well's pump will work but we won't have lights."

"Should we take Sister Grace's body back to the lodge?"

"I don't think that would be a good idea. She was burned pretty severely."

LaNora looked past Noah, into the shed. She thought she could see Grace's body lying on the concrete floor but it was too dark to be certain.

"What a horrible way to die," she said and turned toward the lodge.

"How's Sister Juanita?"

"I don't know. Her hands appear to have been burned pretty bad, though."

"There's a first aid kit in the hall closet. I'll get it."

When the two came into the sitting room, Victoria and Juanita were not there. LaNora felt a rush of dread sweep over her. She turned and rushed up the stairs.

"Victoria!" she called out. "Victoria, where are you?"

When she reached the top of the stairs, she held onto the banister and looked up and down the hall. "Victoria!" she screamed.

The bathroom door opened and Victoria stepped into the hall. "Sister LaNora, what is it?"

LaNora rushed her and threw her arms around her. "Oh, thank God, you're okay."

"Of course I am," Victoria said and patted LaNora's back, signaling it was time to let go. LaNora held onto her and sobbed.

"When I didn't see you downstairs, I thought. . ."

"It's all right. Sister Juanita needed to get cleaned up and change her clothes, that's all. We're fine."

LaNora gradually regained her composure and released Victoria. "Grace is dead," she said and wiped the tears from her cheeks with a handkerchief from her pocket.

"I know," she said, nodding her head. "I need to get back to help Sister Juanita. Her hands are pretty burned. She'll need a doctor to look at them."

"You still think we are going to get out of here?"

"Of course I do. We have to," Victoria said. She tried to sound convinced but LaNora could see the uncertainty and fear in Victoria's eyes.

Moments later, in the sitting room, Juanita lay back on the sofa while Victoria finished bandaging her wounded hands. Noah put another log on the fire and the flames leaped up in approval. LaNora carefully set a tray with a teapot and four cups down on the table.

"Thank heaven for a propane stove," LaNora said. "I figured we could use some hot tea."

"Actually, I could go for something a bit stronger," Noah said, "but tea is fine."

"Why? Why would she want to hurt me?" Juanita asked. "I never did anything to her."

"I don't know," Victoria said.

"What do you mean she tried to kill you?" LaNora asked. "What happened out there?"

"LaNora!" Victoria said.

"It's okay, Mother," Juanita said.

LaNora and Victoria exchanged concerned glances.

"I had just finished getting the generator working and was about to close up the electrical panel. I noticed Sister Grace's shadow. She was behind me holding something over her head. I quickly turned around and jumped out of the way. She threw a large metal can at my head but it hit the generator instead and exploded, knocking me to the ground and throwing Sister Grace against the back of the shed. When I got to my feet, I saw her lying on the floor. Her clothes were on fire. I grabbed my cape and tried to put the fire out but my cape started burning. It was awful." Juanita began to sob. "Why would she do that?"

"She didn't say anything?" LaNora asked and ignored Victoria's glare.

"No. When she was on fire she just kept screaming for her father." Tears ran down the sides of Juanita's face.

"Try not to think about it right now," Victoria said. "Here, have some tea."

"I don't know if I can drink anything," Juanita said. "My throat is so sore."

"Smoke," Noah said.

"I'll get some honey," LaNora said and hurried back to the kitchen. She glanced at the oven. It was still not working. She grabbed the jar of honey from the cupboard and returned to the sitting room. "Here." She handed the jar to Victoria.

Victoria took a teaspoon full and turned to Juanita. "Here, try this," she said and fed it to Juanita. "Let it dissolve slowly in your mouth." She set the spoon back on the tray. "I need to tend to things in the kitchen. Sister LaNora could you give me a hand?"

"Yes, Sister."

"Mr. Talbot, could you show me that thing in the

kitchen?" Victoria said.

LaNora saw the puzzled look on Noah's face. She looked at him and silently prodded him by nodding her head repeatedly but ever so slightly so Juanita would not see.

"Oh, yes," he finally said.

"We'll be right back," LaNora assured Juanita before following Victoria and Noah to the kitchen.

"What is going on?" Victoria asked pressing the palms of her hands against the top of the island. "First, Sister Abigail, then Sister Dominica, and now this."

"It's as I suspected. Sister Grace is behind this," LaNora said.

"But why? Who is she and what connection does she have with Ronnie, if, in fact, this is about Ronnie?"

"I don't know," LaNora said.

"I can tell you this," Noah said. "She wasn't working alone."

Victoria turned her head sharply and looked at the groundskeeper. "And you know this because?"

"Remember the van? She's not strong enough to drag that driver away."

"True," Victoria said and then a pensive look came over her. "It makes sense because last night I heard two people in the attic."

Noah looked at LaNora with a fearful expression.

"What?" Victoria asked looking at him and then LaNora.

LaNora turned to Victoria and lowered her gaze. "Uh, Sister, when you heard someone in the attic," she said with a bit of trepidation. "It was me. I couldn't sleep and I broke into the office to search the desk for any clue as to who the owner is. I found a secret passage with a staircase that led to the attic on the other side of the wall from the girl's bedroom."

"But I heard a man's voice," Victoria objected and looked at Noah.

"That would have been me," he reluctantly admitted.

Victoria looked at LaNora and then at Noah and then back at LaNora. Her disapproval was loud and clear without her saying a word.

"We found a cot in the corner. Someone has been sleeping up there."

"Sister Grace?" Victoria said. It was clear in her tone and pursed lips that she was still upset about the two of them being alone, again.

"No, I don't think so," LaNora answered. "I think it was the person she was working with."

"And why is that?" Victoria asked.

"The trap. Sister Juanita said she wasn't able to open it. If she couldn't, I seriously doubt Sister Grace could have. It would take a stronger person, forgive me, a man," Noah said.

Victoria turned around and looked out the window. "So, there's still someone out there."

"It seems so," LaNora said.

"Oh dear, God," Victoria said, tilting her head back and looking at the ceiling. "How much more do we have to endure?" She looked down and the room fell silent.

"Who would be helping her?" Victoria said in a softer tone that sounded like defeat.

"That I couldn't say. I didn't know her well enough," LaNora answered.

"Maybe Sister Juanita will know," Victoria said, sounding as though she caught a second wind. "Mr. Talbot, how long with that emergency generator work?"

"It depends, if it's not tampered with it should run a long time, but if someone has been messing with it. . . "

"I understand," Victoria nodded. "Let's return to the sitting room and see what Sister Juanita knows."

Back in the sitting room, they found Juanita was sitting up in a chair closer to the heat from the fire. She had the blanket from the back of the sofa across her lap. Sister LaNora sat down on the sofa across from her. Noah sat in the chair.

"Sister, what do you know of Sister Grace? I mean of her life before she came to the Abbey?" Victoria asked, walking over to the window and looking out across the driveway at the snow-covered field.

Juanita looked at the three of them and then back at Victoria. "Why?"

"We think she may have been behind what happened to Sister Abigail and Sister Dominica, but we also think she may have been working with someone else."

Juanita's eyes widened. She swallowed and started to put her hand to her face but stopped when she saw the bandages. "I don't know a whole lot. We talked a few times. She told me she is—was raised an only child. Her mother ran off when she was quite young and her father raised her."

"Did she ever mention his name?" LaNora asked.

Juanita shook her head. "No. She just called him papa when she talked about him."

"Well, we know that the owner at least had one daughter who died and a son," LaNora said. "The attic belonged to a little girl and Sister Victoria, your room was decorated for a boy." She looked at Noah.

"In the time I've been here, no one has never come around, or if they did, they didn't tell me their connection to this place. Like I said before, the owner lets a lot of people stay here."

"Maybe this has nothing to do with the owner," Victoria said. "Maybe it was someone who rented the place."

"The only way to find out is to ask Rothenberg, but we have no way of contacting him," Noah said.

LaNora let out a frustrated groan. "I don't believe this.

In this day and age of electronics and instant communication who would ever want to stay in a place like this?"

"You'd be surprised," Noah said. "A lot of people come here to unplug and reconnect with each other."

"But there has to be something in case of an emergency," LaNora said.

"Usually people still have their cars and can drive out, but to be honest, there hasn't been any urgent need—"

"Until now," Victoria interrupted. She turned back to the window. LaNora watched Victoria's head tilt to the side, the way it did when Victoria has thought of something.

"What is it?" LaNora asked.

Victoria turned back around. "Mr. Talbot, you mentioned neighbors earlier. Do you think they might be there now?" she asked.

"No. They tend to go away for the winter." A grin spread across his lips. "But they do keep a quad in their barn."

"What if we were to sneak out of here after dark and you were to take us there?" Victoria interrupted him.

LaNora felt a glimmer of hope begin to blossom in her chest.

"No," Noah said, squashing the idea and the budding hope.

"Why not?" LaNora asked in a demanding tone.

"Because in your black habits you would stick out like a sore thumb against the snow, even in the dark. If there is someone still out there wishing to do you—us harm, we'd be easy targets."

"You have a point," Victoria said, sounding a bit less enthused.

"Mr. Talbot, what if we covered ourselves with white sheets?" Juanita asked. "You said it yourself, that you couldn't see Sister Grace when she was wrapped in her white cape."

"It still wouldn't work. There would be too many of

us. We'd still be spotted."

"What if you were to go alone?" Victoria asked.

"No!" LaNora said sharply.

"Why not?" Victoria asked.

LaNora opened her mouth to say something but looked at Noah and then back at Victoria.

"I could make better time and go for help," Noah said. "Afterall, I know the area and another way to get there that is better covered."

LaNora felt an unseen hand gripping her heart and squeezing it. She wanted to object that it was too dangerous but she knew she did not dare.

"You could wrap yourself in a sheet or two and—"

"Okay, I'll do it," he said, interrupting Victoria.

"Splendid," Victoria said.

Outside, a guttural scream, like a wounded animal, startled Victoria. She quickly moved away from the window. The other three leaped to their feet.

"What on earth?" LaNora said.

Noah brushed past her and headed toward the kitchen. The others quickly followed. The kitchen was dark. Noah bumped into a stool but caught it before it hit the floor. The four huddled close and looked through the window over the sink. They watched in the dim light above the shed as a man emerged carrying the burned and blackened body of Grace in his arms. He looked heavenward and let out another scream of pain. Then he appeared to look directly at them.

"I'll kill you all!" he shouted from the depth of his soul. He stood for a moment longer and then turned around and disappeared into the woods behind the shed.

"Where's he going?" Juanita asked.

"I don't know," Noah answered.

LaNora felt weak.

"I think I should go now," Noah said. "While he's

preoccupied. I could get over the hill before he could see me."

"No!" LaNora said, sounding frightened.

"I have to. This is our best shot. Now we know where he is, or at least the direction he went."

"But he could come back."

"I'll slip out the back and then head into the woods. I'll be safe. I'll stay low and move quickly," Noah explained while all four of them headed back into the lodge.

"I'll get you a sheet," Victoria said.

"There's no time," Noah said.

They followed Noah to the side door at the end of the hall by the cellar door. He turned back around to look at them. LaNora was worried and afraid for him, but he seemed fearless.

"I'll be back with help. I promise," he said and winked at her.

LaNora started to step forward to hug him but Victoria grabbed her by the arm and held her back.

"God's speed, Mr. Talbot," Victoria said.

Noah nodded and then turned around and in an instant was gone.

"Come, Sisters, we need to make sure the house is secure. Sister LaNora, check the upstairs. Make sure the windows are all locked and lock all of the bedroom doors to the hall."

"What about the doors at the end of the halls? They have glass windows?"

"Right, find something and put it in front of them. Do what you can. Go! Sister Juanita, go to the kitchen and keep a lookout in case that man returns."

"Yes, Sister," Juanita said and rushed away with her bandaged hands held up in front of her.

Upstairs, LaNora quickly pulled the armoire from the empty bedroom nearest the end of the hall. It was heavy but she managed it alone. She attributed it to her fear and the rush of adrenaline it gave her. Once it was in place in front of the locked outside door, she began making sure the windows and doors were locked. When she came to Sister Grace's room, she remembered the secret passageway. She tried to move the armoire but when she did, the door behind the bookcase began to open. She quickly closed the secret door and grabbed ahold of the bed. Dragging it across the room she tipped it up on its end, letting the mattress fall against the bookcase. As an added measure to slow down an intruder, she slid the writing desk up against the underside of the wooden bed frame. Winded, but feeling safer, she continued locking the rest of the bedroom doors.

"Upstairs is secure," she said when she returned to the foyer.

"Splendid. I have secured the first floor as best as can be."

"Sisters!" Juanita called out.

Victoria and LaNora hurried into the kitchen.

"I just saw something move in the woods over there." She pointed on the opposite side of the shed, away from the path to Noah's cabin where the stranger had gone moments ago. "I think he was heading deeper into the woods."

"Oh no!" LaNora gasped. "Noah."

The crack of a rifle going off caused the three to jump back and nearly fall to the floor.

Juanita and Victoria crossed themselves.

"No!" LaNora screamed. She rushed to the kitchen door.

"LaNora, stop!" Victoria shouted.

The sound of another gunshot halted her. Victoria grabbed LaNora and pulled her away from the door before she could open it.

"No," she whimpered and collapsed to the floor,

weeping.

"It's going to be okay," Victoria said, holding LaNora tightly in her arms. "Mr. Talbot knows these woods better than anyone. He'll be fine."

A third gunshot echoed off the hills and trees. It sounded more distant. Victoria felt LaNora's body tense.

"What are we going to do?" Juanita asked.

"There's nothing we can do but pray that Mr. Talbot makes it to the neighbors."

The timer on the stove went off, sending Juanita to the floor.

"Oh, sweet Jesus," Victoria said. She let go of LaNora and rushed to turn off the buzzer. She returned to LaNora who sat weeping into her hands. "Sister," she said firmly, "get a hold of yourself. We have things to do."

LaNora nodded and climbed to her feet.

"Mr. Talbot is going to be okay," Victoria said, trying to sound positive, but her expression said she was not so sure.

The lodge grew darker as night approached. It had been several hours since the sisters had heard the gunshots. In the sitting room, the three huddled close on the floor in front of the fire, their backs to the sofa. The drapes on the windows were pulled closed and the bookcases had been placed in front of them. In the silence, LaNora could not think of anything but Noah.

"Do you think he made it?" she whispered.

"It's in God's hands now," Victoria answered while slipping another rosary bead between her finger and thumb.

LaNora turned to look across the foyer into the dining room. The emergency lights in the foyer made it impossible to see anything clearly. She turned around.

"He has to be all right," she said.

"Sister, please," Victoria said in a chastising tone.

"Your time would be better spent praying."

"But I can't. I can't sit here and do nothing."

"Praying is not nothing," Victoria said. "Besides, what can we do?"

"There are guns in the office," LaNora said through clenched teeth.

"Guns?" Juanita said. "Oh no, we couldn't."

"Under normal circumstances, I would agree with you, but this isn't normal. There is someone out there intent on killing us. We can't let him."

"Sister, we can not take a life," Victoria said. "It is a mortal sin for which could result in eternal damnation."

"I don't mean to kill him," LaNora said. "Just stop him from killing us."

"He who lives by the sword perishes by the sword. Matthew, chapter twenty-six, verse fifty-two," Victoria said and another bead slipped through her fingers.

"I don't care," LaNora said. "I'm going to go crazy just sitting here. We have to do something." She stood up and began to pace.

"Sister, please, sit down," Juanita said. "You're making me nervous."

LaNora stopped pacing. "I'm sorry," she said and sat down in the chair beside the hearth.

Another hour passed. The fire burned down to embers.

"We need more wood for the fire," LaNora said.

"No," Victoria snapped. "He could be waiting. It's too risky."

LaNora settled back in her chair and stuck her hands in the opposite sleeves of her habit. The room grew darker. Victoria looped her rosary around her belt.

"What are we going to do?" Juanita asked.

"I feel like we're sitting ducks," LaNora said.

"I know. Surely Mr. Talbot should have reached the

neighbor's cabin by now."

"How long do you think it will take for help to come from Pendleton?" Juanita asked.

"It took us just a half-hour from the time we turned off I-84," Victoria said.

A loud thud at the front door caused the three to jump. LaNora's hands covered her mouth to stifle a scream. Her heart beat faster. Once the silence returned, she lowered her hands.

"What was that?" Juanita whispered.

"Stay here," Victoria said. She slowly stood up.

"What are you doing?" LaNora asked and stood.

"Just stay here," Victoria repeated firmly. Carefully she made her way around the end of the sofa and inched her way closer to the foyer.

LaNora helped Juanita to her feet and the pair moved to the corner of the sitting room where LaNora could get a clearer view of the foyer.

"Sister, be careful," she said to Victoria.

Victoria turned and looked at her with her finger pressed against her lips. Turning back toward the front door, she tiptoed closer to the door.

"I don't like this," Juanita whispered.

LaNora left Juanita and inched her way toward the sofa so she could keep Victoria in sight. She watched as Victoria put her ear against the door. LaNora glanced into the dining room, at the window on the far wall. It was dark outside but the snow cover reflected the glow of the security lights at the end of the lodge. "Oh, Noah, where are you?" she said under her breath.

"I don't hear anything," Victoria whispered and turned away from the door.

Without warning a loud explosion shook the lodge. LaNora fell to the floor. Juanita was thrown back against the corner. LaNora, ears ringing, scrambled to her knees. Cold air blew dust and smoke into the sitting room. Through it, LaNora spotted Victoria lying face down on the foyer floor among fragments of the wooden doors.

"No, no, no," LaNora said and started to stand up but the sound of heavy footsteps entering the lodge sent her diving to the floor in front of the sofa. She glanced at Juanita who was standing in the corner, her white bandaged hands and the white of her wimple were bright against the black of her habit. LaNora motioned for her to get down but Juanita's attention was on something in the foyer.

"No. No. Please, senor," Juanita pleaded.

"You murdering bitch, this is for Ronnie," the deep raspy voice of a man said.

The loud crack of a rifle thundered throughout the lodge. Juanita was thrown back against the wall. Another shot and she slid down the wall to the floor. LaNora covered her mouth with her hands and turned her face to the floor.

The gunman's footsteps moved deeper into the lodge. LaNora heard the kitchen door hit the wall as it was pushed open. She waited until it closed. Quickly she crawled across the room toward the corner between the door and the window and pressed her back against the wall and stayed low. "Oh dear God, please don't let him kill me," she prayed in an undertone.

The sound of the footsteps returned to the foyer, LaNora pressed herself against the wall harder and hoped the room was dark enough to hide her. Her heart was beating loudly in her ears. She closed her eyes and listened. Moments later, she heard the man upstairs, but he was not breaking down the doors. The realization hit her that he must have keys to the rooms. The sound of the man stomping down the stairs caused LaNora to hold her breath.

"Come out, come out wherever you are," the man sang out. "She has to be around here somewhere. Oh, did she sneak outside? Don't worry. I'll find your friend and send her along shortly. You can all rot in hell."

The footsteps moved outside. LaNora could hear him outside the window above her. She held her breath and did not move. The sound of snow crunching beneath the man's feet began faded into the distance. LaNora lay trembling, crying, and praying.

CHAPTER TWELVE

LaNora woke with a start. Slowly she sat up. The room was cold. Her breath made momentary white clouds in front of her face. Looking across the room she saw the fire had burned completely out. Her eyes wandered to the corner. The wall was smeared with blood. She followed it down to where Juanita's body was slumped over like a ragdoll. Tears filled LaNora's eyes.

A stirring in the foyer caused LaNora to flatten herself against the wall. She listened. A faint groaning drifted into the room. LaNora's eyes widened as she recognized the sound. She crawled out of her hiding place to take a better look.

Still sprawled face-down on the floor, Victoria pulled her hands back. She pressed her palms against the floor and tried to push herself to her knees but only managed to raise an inch before collapsing again. "Sisters," she said in a weak, faint voice.

LaNora crawled to the doorway of the sitting room. A gust of cold air blew through the gaping hole where the front doors had been. LaNora looked outside to be sure the gunman was not waiting with his shotgun ready to fire on them. He was nowhere to be seen. She turned to Victoria and took her hand.

"Oh thank the Lord you're alive," she said and kissed Victoria's hand.

Victoria turned her head and looked up. "LaNora?"

"Yes, it's me. Are you hurt?"

"I don't think so," Victoria said and rolled onto her side. "What happened?"

"There was an explosion. Can you stand?"

"Give me your hand."

LaNora held out her hand but Victoria ignored her. She turned back over and pushed herself up then pulled the skirt of her habit up so she could kneel. Once on all fours, she reached for LaNora's hand and pulled herself to her feet. Immediately she fell against LaNora.

"Are you okay?" she asked, looking at Victoria's dazed eyes.

"A little dizzy and my back hurts a bit but I think I'll be all right. Where's Sister Juanita?"

LaNora looked over her shoulder toward the sitting room and then turned back to Victoria. "She's dead."

"Dead?" Victoria repeated and looked confused.

"After the explosion, that man came in. I tried to get her to duck down and hide but he saw her and shot her."

"No. Not, Juanita." Victoria groaned and started to weep.

LaNora glanced at the hole in the wall. "We can't stay here. He'll be back. We have to hide," she said. Her eyes scanned the rubble on the floor and spotted their capes. She let go of Victoria's hand and pulled the capes free. Wrapping one around Victoria's shoulder and then donning hers, she took Victoria's arm. "Come with me. I know a place."

LaNora led Victoria down the hall to the office.

"Your keys?" she said and held out her hand.

Victoria looked confused.

"In your pocket, remember?"

"Oh, yes." Victoria pulled out the keyring and handed it to LaNora.

"The gunman didn't look in here," she said while she

unlocked the office door.

Once inside the room, LaNora closed the door and locked it. Turning around, she glanced at the gun cabinet, at the rifles lined up with their muzzles pointed at the ceiling. The urge to grab the one that resembled the gun her father taught her to shoot pulled at her, but Sister Victoria needed her help and they needed to hide.

LaNora hastened to the bookcase and reached for the book on the top shelf that was the latch to the secret passage. The click of the latch coming undone seemed louder and LaNora cringed. Cautiously she opened the bookcase to reveal the spiral staircase inside.

LaNora did not say a word but pointed down. Victoria stepped onto the landing and then grabbed the handrails on the staircase to steady herself. She slowly backed down the stairs as though it were a ladder. LaNora gently pushed the door closed and heard the latch secure it. She looked for something to jam the door with but, seeing nothing, she followed Victoria to the bottom of the stairs.

At the bottom of the stairwell was another door. Instead of a doorknob, it had a gate latch at the top. LaNora reached up and as quietly as she could, opened it. The door, like the office's, opened toward her. She gripped the edge with her fingertips and pulled. Surprisingly, it swung open with ease. On the inside side of the door were shelves of wine bottles. She motioned for Victoria to go inside. A bit more steady on her feet, Victoria did as instructed. LaNora followed and pulled the door closed.

The light in the wine cellar was dim. The batteries in the emergency lights had begun to fail. LaNora took stock of the room. It was larger than she had expected but having never been in a wine cellar, she was not exactly sure how big a wine cellar would be. The room was wider than the office above, of that she was certain. She guessed it was under the hallway above as well as the office. All four walls were made of red bricks and lined with shelves and stocked with bottles of wine.

In the center of the room were stacks of boxes of vodka, whiskey, and other assorted liquors. *This is too much for a normal household,* LaNora thought.

"Sister, why is this happening? Who is this man?" Victoria asked, breaking the silence.

LaNora cringed at how loud Victoria's voice was. She motioned for her to be quiet.

"I don't know for sure but I think he might be related to Ronnie somehow," LaNora whispered. "Last night, before he shot Sister Juanita, he said something about Ronnie."

"We didn't do anything. Ronnie was mentally unstable."

"I know that, but for some reason he blames us."

"What about Sister Grace? Did he say how she's connected to all of this?"

"No."

Victoria staggered and sat down on an unopened box of liquor.

"I do hope that No—Mr. Talbot made it and returns with help soon," LaNora said and turned away from Victoria.

"As do I. What are you doing?" Victoria asked.

"Looking for a place to hide in case that man comes down here."

"Do you think he will?"

"I don't know," LaNora said. "Maybe this was a bad idea. There is no place for us to hide."

"What if we turned off the light? We could pull a shelf away from the wall and hide behind it?"

"No. I don't like this," LaNora said. "We would still be trapped. We need a place that would give us a way out."

LaNora began to pace. Victoria put a hand to her head and took an unsteady breath.

"Are you sure you're all right?" LaNora asked.

"I could use some ibuprofen. My head is killing me."

"I saw some in the kitchen cupboard," LaNora said.

"No," Victoria said and held up her hand as though to say stop. "I don't trust anything in this house anymore. I brought some in my bag that's in my room."

"We'll get it, then," LaNora said.

"How?"

"The secret passageway. It has a door into Sister Grace's room."

LaNora walked back to the corner where they had entered. Remembering the book-trigger upstairs in the office, she looked at the bottles on the top shelf. Reaching up, she began pulling out the bottles of wine until one bottle on the left pulled back.

"I found you," she said and was about to pull harder when she heard a noise above them. She let go of the bottle and stood back.

The footsteps stopped above Victoria. She jumped to her feet and moved away from the boxes, keeping her eyes on the ceiling.

"This way," LaNora whispered and pulled Victoria toward the main entrance of the cellar. Her heart was racing. They stood by the door and listened.

The footsteps entered the office above. LaNora put her hand on the doorknob and gently turned it. When they heard the sound of the bookcase above move, she opened the door and motioned for Victoria to go.

Like the stairs to the attic, a staircase to the main floor was on the other side of the door. LaNora followed Victoria and quietly closed the door behind her. She felt for a lock but there was none. Victoria moved up the stairs quietly, and LaNora followed. When they reached to top, Victoria took the keys from her pocket and unlocked the door.

A blast of cold air struck LaNora when she entered the hallway on the main floor. She looked beside her at the back door that led outside. The window had been blown out. She tapped Victoria on the shoulder to get her attention. Victoria turned around.

"Outside," LaNora mouthed the word. She opened the door and slipped into the cold.

Once they both were outside, Victoria closed the door and stood beside LaNora, leaning against the outside wall of the lodge.

The snow was falling. LaNora guessed that it had been for a long time since she could not see any footprints. If they were to run, the weight of their cape dragging across the snow could conceal their footprints. She motioned for Victoria to follow her.

Stealthily she crept to the front of the lodge and peeked around the corner. There was no sign of the gunman. She listened but could not hear a thing. She started to move around the corner but Victoria grabbed her arm and pulled her back.

"What are you doing?" she whispered.

"We need to get to the neighbor's house."

"No!"

"We have to get help," she said and pointing at the snow.

"He'll see us if we go that way."

LaNora thought for a moment. "You're right," she said. "We can try to go the way Mr. Talbot went."

LaNora turned back toward the opposite corner. When she reached the door, she stopped and listened. A sound deep in the lodge caused her to flatten herself against the side of the lodge.

"What is it?" Victoria asked, standing beside LaNora.

"I heard the gunman. I think he's upstairs," LaNora said. Cautiously she peeked through the broken window. She could see straight through to the staircase. There was no sign of the gunman.

The two made their way to the back corner of the lodge. The upper deck wrapped around the entire lodge, shielding the windows above from their view but also hiding them from the possibility of the gunman seeing them.

"If we make a run for the trees this way," LaNora said, making a line with her arm from the corner of the lodge at an angle away toward the trees, "We'll have a better chance of not being seen. Make sure your cape drags in the snow."

"Okay," Victoria said with a bit of hesitation.

"On three," LaNora said and counted it out.

The pair ran as quickly as they could across the deep snow. When they reached the trees, LaNora stopped and looked back. Their skirts and capes had dragged across the surface of the snow but they did not quite fill in their footprints. However, in a few minutes, the falling snow would finish the job.

"Come on," she said and turned around. "We need to go this way."

The branches of the trees helped keep the snow from building up on the ground beneath and made it easier for them to put some distance between them and the lodge. Still, Victoria began to lag behind. LaNora stopped and turned back.

"Sister, how's your head?" she asked as she took hold of Victoria's arm.

"It's still there," she said and grimaced. "What I wouldn't do for an ibuprofen."

"I'm sorry."

"Oh, I'll be all right. We should keep going."

"I think we are far enough away we don't need to run," LaNora said, looking back toward the lodge but not seeing it.

They continued through the woods.

The trees began to get shorter and thinner the closer they came to the top of the hill. LaNora remembered the fire and wondered if they were getting near.

"I need to rest," Victoria said, trying to catch her breath. "I can't go on."

LaNora stopped and looked around for someplace to get out of the weather. She spotted what appeared to be a shed not too far away.

"Do you think you could make it?" she asked Victoria.

Victoria eyed the structure. It was several yards away. She took a deep breath. "I think so," she said.

The shed turned out to be a three-sided structure. LaNora remembered her father once talked about hunters who would build a lean-to type structure and camouflage it so the game would not spot them. She thought it was not fair to the animals. They should be allowed to have a fighting chance against humans with guns. LaNora wondered if this structure was one of those. As much as she hated them, at that moment, she was glad it was there.

"Here, sit down here," she said, directing Victoria into a dry corner of the shelter. "I'm going to scout on ahead. Not too far. I want to see if I can spot the neighbors' cabin."

"No," Victoria said and grabbed hold of LaNora's arm. "Stay with me."

LaNora looked at Victoria. There was something different in her eyes, a look she had never seen before. It frightened LaNora.

"I'll stay," she said and sat down beside Victoria.

"Thank you," Victoria said and leaned against LaNora.

LaNora let her eyes close and in no time fell asleep.

The crack of a breaking tree branch and the thud of the heavy snow hitting the ground startled LaNora awake. She looked around. The snow was deeper but there was something else. It was faint. LaNora cocked her head and listened.

Her eyes widened when she recognized the familiar sound of crunching snow. She nudged Victoria who was still asleep, her head resting on LaNora's shoulder.

"Sister," she whispered. "Wake up. We need to get moving."

Victoria opened her eyes and sat up. "What?"

"Shh," LaNora shushed, putting a finger to her lips the way she did when her pupils were too noisy.

"What is it?" Victoria whispered, still a bit groggy.

"We need to get moving. I heard something coming," LaNora said and stood up. She held out her hand to Victoria and pulled her to her feet.

"How far away?"

"I'm not sure. It sounded faint so I'm guessing far, but we

don't want him getting any closer. Come on."

LaNora led the way out of the shelter and continued toward the peak. The snow was deeper the closer they came to the crest of the hill.

"Mr. Talbot showed me the neighbor's cabin is on the other side of the burn. Their property was spared," LaNora said, more to reassure herself than Victoria. "Once we get to the top, we should be able to see it."

"I ho—"

The sound of barking echoing off the surrounding hills brought them to their knees. LaNora looked back toward the direction of the lodge, where she thought the sound came from. Something moved several yards back. She strained to see if it were real or just imagined. Her pulse quickened but there was nothing. She looked ahead at the barren hilltop. They had reached the burn.

"Find them, Scout," a man yelled.

"Oh dear God," Victoria said, her eyes wide with fear. "I know we aren't supposed to hate, but I hate dogs."

LaNora searched the hillside in front of them. They were almost to the burn.

"Come on," she said and began running.

Victoria followed her, staying close.

The dog began to bark wildly and sounded as if it were getting closer. Neither looked back until they reached the crest and the edge of the burn. LaNora saw the dark figure of the animal bounding through the forest toward them.

"Which way do we go?" Victoria asked.

LaNora turned around. The snow was coming down in large flakes making it hard to see.

Suddenly the high-pitched shriek of an animal in pain pierced the silence and echoed all around them.

"Scout!" the man yelled. "God damn it!"

LaNora looked back and saw the dog thrashing about on the ground a good distance away. She remembered the trap that Dominica had stepped on and shuddered. Looking back at the hillside she spotted a cluster of mountain pine bushes a few yards down the hillside.

"There!" she said. "We can hide behind those."

The snow was nearly a foot deep. LaNora's stockings were no match for the bitter cold and damp. Every step became painful, and she felt as though she were walking on needles. She said a silent prayer and pushed on.

They reached the shrubs and ducked behind them. LaNora prayed that their dragging skirts and capes, plus the falling snow had buried their tracks enough to keep them safe. Then she noticed her breath, a bellowing fog cloud that hung in the air.

"Breath through your cape, Sister," she said.

Victoria looked puzzled but then realized why. She quickly complied.

LaNora peered through the snow-covered branches of the bush toward the top of the hill. She gasped and grabbed Victoria's arm when a dark figure appeared at the crest. He was dressed in a long, dark duster and a snow-covered western hat. *He looked every part the image of a cowboy on the range,* LaNora thought, down to the rifle he held in his hands.

"I know you're out there," he shouted into the air. "You think you're pretty clever, pretending to be dead. I should have shot you anyway. My mistake. It won't happen again."

LaNora looked at Victoria who was visibly shaken by his words. She put a reassuring hand on Victoria's arm and gave her a look that said, do not listen to him.

"You might as well give up now," he continued, letting his voice echo through the hills. "You'll never get away, just ask that boyfriend of yours. That's right, I saw the two of you."

LaNora gasped and closed her eyes. She felt Victoria looking at her.

"I didn't think nuns were supposed to do that," the man continued. "Naughty, naughty. I wonder what Mother Superior would have to say about that. I bet you'll have to say more than ten Hail Marys."

LaNora glanced at Victoria. "Later," she mouthed.

The man stood still, looking off in the distance, not looking in their direction. Then, without warning, he turned around and retreated into the woods.

The two waited and watched until he was out of sight. They started to get to their feet when they heard the dog shriek again. Then a blast from a shotgun.

"Come on," LaNora said and helped Victoria to her feet. "We need to find a better place to hide until it gets dark."

CHAPTER THIRTEEN

At the bottom of the hillside, they sheltered in a small pumphouse that was no bigger than a broom closet but at least was dry inside. There was also heat from a sunlamp the neighbors used to keep the pump from freezing. LaNora stood by the door, peeking out through the crack between the boards. The snow had stopped falling and it was getting dark. She looked at Victoria who was curled up on the dirt floor. They had not said a word to each other since the man made his announcement. LaNora was not sure what to say.

The sound of a rifle being shot startled Victoria awake.

"LaNora?" she said, still groggy.

"I'm right here," she answered and tried to see through the cracks in the wall that faced the hillside. "It's okay, I don't see anyone out there. We'll wait until it gets dark and then make our way to the neighbor's cabin."

"Okay," Victoria said and settled back down.

LaNora turned back to watching through the cracks in the door and retreated into her thoughts. The man's words kept echoing in her memory. "You'll never get away, just ask your boyfriend." *Oh God, please let him be lying. Let Noah still be alive. Let him have escaped this nightmare and gone for help. I promise I'll keep my vow. I won't leave the Abbey. Just let him be alive.* "Please."

"What?" Victoria asked.

LaNora cringed. She had not realized she had spoken. She looked at Victoria. "Nothing, Sister. I was just thinking out loud."

"Bartering with God?" Victoria asked.

"You always could tell what I was thinking."

"God doesn't work like that, Sister."

"I know," LaNora said and looked away from Victoria. "I just keep thinking about what that man said about Mr. Talbot—"

"Your boyfriend?" Victoria said.

LaNora looked at her again.

"What did he mean by that?"

LaNora felt her cheeks begin to blush. She felt ashamed and for a split-second thought of a lie. "He kissed me," she said.

Victoria nodded. "I see. Did you kiss him back?"

"It all—yes, I did."

Victoria climbed to her feet and stood in the opposite corner of the small pumphouse. "It was a onetime thing. These are extenuating circumstances—"

"It happened two more times after that," LaNora said, interrupting Victoria's attempt to rationalize the situation.

Victoria looked at her without saying a word.

"I was wrong. It was my fault. I should never have let myself be alone with him and I tried not to be but—"

"It's not all on you," Victoria said. "He shares some of the blame."

"No, if I hadn't pried into his personal life, if I would have just kept my distance and not lowered my guard—"

"Sister, what-ifs are a waste of time and energy. What happened, happened. There's nothing that can be done about it now. We need to stay focused and figure out a way to get out of here."

"I promise, Sister, I have no intention of leaving the order. I made a vow and I intend on keeping it."

"I'm happy to hear that. Now, what's our plan?"

The light outside grew dark. LaNora waited and listened. It felt as though it had been hours since they entered the pumphouse. Her habit felt dry.

"I think we can go now," she said. "I don't see any signs of the man."

"Do you think he shot his dog?" Victoria asked.

"I don't know but I haven't heard the dog since."

"I know it's uncharitable and we are supposed to love all of God's creatures but I can't stand dogs."

"Why?" LaNora asked.

"When I was a young girl, our neighbors had a German Shepherd. It was mean and so was the neighbor. My younger brother and I were playing catch in the backyard. The ball went over the fence. I looked to see if the dog was out but didn't see it. The ball wasn't too far from the fence. So, I climbed over the fence. I grabbed the ball and yelled to my brother to let him know I had it. That must have awakened the dog and he came out of his doghouse. I threw the ball over the fence and started to climb but the dog was quick. He bit my leg and tried to pull me back into the yard. I kicked him with my other foot until he eventually let go. I made it back across the fence but my leg was hurt pretty bad. I still have scars from that dog's teeth."

"I'm sorry," LaNora said.

"Oh don't be. It was my fault. I shouldn't have gone in their yard. Besides, the dog died years ago."

"But you are still afraid of them."

"True," Victoria said.

"Ready to go?" LaNora asked after taking another look outside.

"Yes."

Slowly LaNora pushed against the wooden door. Outside, fresh snow had built up against it since they entered.

She pushed with her foot as well and the door began to open. Once outside, LaNora quickly closed the door before there was any chance of someone seeing the light from inside.

"Where to?" Victoria whispered.

"This way," LaNora said.

They headed south along the tree line where the snow was less deep. "We should be getting close," LaNora said and suddenly her foot slipped from under her. She caught herself before she could fall.

"Ice, Sister. Be careful," she warned and took Victoria's hand.

Victoria inched her way closer to LaNora. The flat soles of her shoes and the wet snow made it hard for her to get any traction. A loud crack split the silence and Victoria's foot dropped through the ice. She let out a muffled groan and tightened its hold on LaNora's hand causing LaNora to wince.

"Are you okay?" LaNora asked.

"My ankle," Victoria answered reaching down and feeling her thigh. "I may have twisted it."

"Oh no," LaNora said. She looked back at the top of the hill. Still nothing. She grabbed ahold of Victoria's arms and pulled her free. The ice continued to break beneath her and she stumbled many times before reaching the bank of the creek.

"Is it unbearable?" LaNora asked.

"Not really. The cold water made it numb."

"Here, lean on me. Let's get to the barn at least and then I'll have a look at it."

It took longer for the two to make the last hundred yards to the large, two-story barn. The main doors were open wide enough for two people to fit through. Without thinking, they went inside.

The barn was dark. The scent of hay, dirt, and motor oil was thick and filled the air. LaNora choked and coughed until she became accustomed to the smell. Feeling the floor with her feet, she found a place for them to sit, a wooden bench to the right of the door sat against a wall. LaNora strained her eyes, trying to force them to see in the darkness but it was no good.

"How's your ankle?" she asked Victoria.

"It hurts."

LaNora knelt down in front of Victoria and blindly felt the injured ankle. "It's not broken," she said. "But I do think it has begun to swell. It should be wrapped." She turned and looked over her shoulder but could not see anything.

When she heard fabric tearing, she looked at Victoria. She had removed her black veil, leaving only her white wimple to cover her head.

"I'm tearing off a couple of strips of my veil for you to use," she answered and handed the piece to LaNora. "May as well remove this, too," she said and undid the laces of her wimple. "I can't walk around looking like a bowling pin."

LaNora gave a quiet laugh while she continued to wrap the strips from the veil around Victoria's shoe and ankle. When she was finished, she stood up. "How's that?"

Victoria gently rose to her feet and took a step. Letting out a soft cry she groped for LaNora and finding her, fell against her. "I don't suppose there are any crutches in here?" she teased.

"We'll have to wait here until morning," LaNora said. "It's too risky to stumble around in the dark. It wouldn't do either of us good if we both injured ourselves."

"True."

LaNora heard the rattle of rosary beads and knew that Victoria had begun to pray silently. She felt the beads looped around her belt and thought about praying but the guilt she felt over Noah, the kiss, and her attempts to barter with God caused her to let go. Instead, her thoughts turned to her children. School would resume the morning after next. They would be coming to class expecting to see her but instead finding a substitute. She knew from experience they would be disappointed. They were a good group of children. She had to make it back, for their sakes. She rose to her feet and took a few steps away from the bench and Victoria.

"What is it, Sister?" Victoria said in her usual kind tone.

"Just thinking," LaNora said.

"About Mr. Talbot?"

"No. My children."

"Oh, yes," Victoria said.

"We have to make it out of here for them."

"And we shall."

LaNora looked up at the darkness above her as she was swallowed up by her emotions. Tears flooded her eyes and spilled from the corners, running down the sides of her face toward her ears. *Oh please, God. Let us make it home to our pupils.*

Victoria slipped her rosary around her belt and stood up. She took a hop-step and finding LaNora, slipped an arm around her shoulders. "We are going to make it. You'll see. You just have to keep your faith strong."

"I think I'm losing my faith, Sister," LaNora said. "I don't think I'm strong enough."

"We're under a severe test," Victoria said. "It's understandable but you *are* strong, Sister. You and I will come through this. You'll see."

LaNora leaned into Victoria's embrace. She felt her anxiety begin to ebb and fade away. They returned to the bench.

LaNora woke with a start. Sunlight shone through the windows and door of the barn, illuminating the inside. She looked at Victoria who was resting her head against the gate of an empty stall behind them. It had been years since LaNora had seen Victoria's rich chestnut hair. It was cut short in an almost manly style. LaNora thought of her own hair, twisted and pinned in a tight bun beneath her wimple. Why had she not cut it short? Was it another sign of her weak faith? She looked away.

The inside of the barn was neatly arranged. Across from them was a workbench with tools and brushes for grooming and maintaining horses. A large anvil sat on a solid round barrel beneath a wall of hammers, rusty pliers with strangely shaped jaws, and pointed spikes resembling long nails. A metal cart with what looked like a small heating stove sat cold beside the anvil. A long, twisted metal poker hung from a hook on the front right leg on the cart. LaNora eyed it and wondered if it would work as a cane for Victoria. She quietly stood up and walked across the center aisle of the barn to it.

The metal of the poker was cold like ice. LaNora nearly dropped it at first. The warmth of her hand began to take the chill off the handle. At the end of the poker were a point and a curved spur. LaNora turned the poker over and put the handle on the ground. She then tested it using the spur as the crook of a cane. She exhaled a discouraged sigh. The poker felt too short. She turned and looked toward the back of the barn.

A mountain of stacked hay bales rose toward the loft. A pitchfork along with well-used, scoop shovels hung on hooks on the wall. LaNora started toward the tools but suddenly stopped and turned around. She scanned the inside of the barn again.

"The quad," she said aloud.

Rushing back to the Victoria, she put her hand on Victoria's shoulder. "Victoria, wake up. We have to go."

Victoria's body spasmed and her head jerked as she opened her eyes. "What is it?"

"Get up, we have to go," LaNora answered and took hold of Victoria's arm to help her to her feet.

"Go? Where?"

"Back to the lodge—"

"Back? Are you joking?" Victoria said and pulled her arm free from LaNora.

"No. We need to get back there."

"Why?"

"The quad, it's gone."

"So?"

"So, Mr. Talbot is still alive. He made it," LaNora said, smiling and with excitement in her tone. "He took the quad to get help."

"But why do we need to go back there?" Victoria said and folded her arms over her chest.

"Because anyone coming to help us will be looking for us there."

"But we don't know how long it will be before help arrives and have you forgotten that is where the man is who is trying to kill us is?"

"No, I haven't forgotten, but it's been over twenty-four hours since Mr. Talbot left."

"I think we should stay. We're safer here," Victoria said while she looked around the barn.

"I know a place where we can hide and be safe and warm until help arrives," LaNora said.

Victoria reacted to the suggestion that she'd be warm by rubbing her arms. "Warm would be nice," she said. "Are you sure we'll be safe?"

"Positive," LaNora said.

"Very well," Victoria said and took a step. Immediately she slumped to the right as pain shot up her leg, reminding her that she had injured her ankle. "Well, this is a problem."

"Here, take this," LaNora said, handing her the poker.

Victoria eyed the metal rod with a crook and point at the end. "And what am I supposed to do with it?"

"See if it will work as a cane. Use the crook as a handle."

Victoria did not appear as sure as LaNora. Hesitantly she turned the poker around and gripped the curved end. She put the handle to the ground. "It's about an inch shorter than ideal, but it might work," she said and tried taking a few steps.

The pain was excruciating and she would have fallen if LaNora had not caught her.

"I'm sorry," LaNora said and looked around for something else. She thought about trying a scoop shovel but it would be too heavy in the snow. "Lean on me. I'll help you," she said.

Victoria handed her the poker and put her arm around LaNora's shoulders. LaNora pulled Victoria closer.

"It'll be like we're in a three-legged race," she said and gave a little chuckle.

"Great, I was never any good at those," Victoria admitted.

Slowly the two made their way to the barn door. The sun was shining bright above them, illuminating the snow, making it blindingly white. LaNora paused until her eyes adjusted to the brightness.

When they reached the creek they stopped.

"I don't think we can or should do this together," Victoria said. "We could both get hurt."

LaNora looked to her right and left and then saw it a few yards away. If only she would have seen it in the dark the night before, she silently lamented. "There's a bridge," she said and pulled Victoria closer. "We'll use it."

They limped along the edge of the creek until they came to the small arched bridge with handrails on either side. Covered in snow, LaNora thought it looked straight out of a Currier and Ives painting.

"Look," Victoria said and pulled back a bit.

LaNora looked at the top of the hill and saw nothing but the tree line and the burned-out cell tower. "What?" she asked.

"There's blood," Victoria said, pointing at the bridge deck.

LaNora looked down. Her chest suddenly felt hollow when she saw the dark-red stained snow.

"He was shot," Victoria said.

"But he still managed to take the quad and get away," she said in an attempt to regain her hope of rescue. "Come on, we have to keep going. We're easy targets against this snow."

Again, the two began moving. Climbing the hill, LaNora felt winded quickly. They took several breaks behind the large mountain pine bushes that dotted the hillside to catch their breaths.

"The hill is a lot steeper than I thought," LaNora said.

When they reached the cell tower, LaNora guided Victoria away from the path and into the woods. The snow was thinner beneath the trees and they would not have to work as hard to walk.

"Mr. Talbot showed me the owner's stone pumphouse," she said as they made their way. "He said the owner installed a heater to keep it from freezing during the winter. It's bigger than the one we stayed in last night. We will be safe there. We can wait and listen for Mr. Talbot and the police."

"Splendid," Victoria said.

"How's your ankle?"

"It still pains me but it's a bit numb again from the cold."

"It's not much further," LaNora said while they hobbled through the woods.

The snow-covered roof of the pumphouse came into view ahead of them.

"There," LaNora said and stopped so Victoria could see for herself.

The silence was shattered by the sputtering sound of an unmuffled engine. It grew louder and closer. LaNora saw movement among the trees in the distance beyond the pumphouse. It was coming toward them. Her heart began to pound faster as fear tightened its grip on her. She looked around and spotted a cluster of shrubs near the base of a large pine tree.

"There," she said and pulled Victoria in the direction

of the shrubs.

When the quad with its driver came into view, they were safely tucked in among the thick branches of the shrubs. They watched as the quad sped along the path toward the crest of the hill and the tower. The driver had a helmet covering his face but LaNora could tell that he was searching the woods as he rode.

"Is it Mr. Talbot?" Victoria asked.

"I don't know," LaNora whispered.

Suddenly the quad skidded to a stop a few yards away from them. The driver stood up from his seat and turned his head away from them. Slowly he scanned the woods to his right and then left.

"Sisters!" he shouted but the helmet muffled his call.

"It's him," Victoria said. Before LaNora could stop her, she crawled out from their hiding place.

"Victoria, stop!" LaNora whispered. She started after her but a branch caught on her habit, stopping her.

"Over here, Mr. Talbot," Victoria cried out and waved at the driver.

He motioned for her to come to him. Before LaNora could free herself from the branch, Victoria began limping away on her own.

"Sister, no," LaNora called to her and gave a final tug on the skirt of her habit to free it. She rushed after Victoria but Victoria had already reached the quad.

"Oh, praise the Lord," Victoria said. "We are so glad to see you." She threw her arms around the driver's neck.

LaNora saw something in the driver's right hand as he hugged Victoria. Suddenly his body stiffened and jerked. Victoria screamed and fell backward onto the ground.

"No!" LaNora screamed and tightened her grip on the handle of the poker. Before she knew what she was doing she swung the hooked end with all her strength. It struck the helmet of the driver with a loud crack, causing him to drop his large, blood-covered, hunting knife at Victoria's feet. He rocked forward over the handlebars but managed to stay on the quad. LaNora struck him again. The helmet split open in the back and the rider's body went limp. He fell to the frozen ground on the opposite side of the quad from Victoria. LaNora's adrenaline coursed through her veins and she raised the poker again, this time aiming for the man's unprotected chest.

"LaNora, no!" Victoria said, gasping and choking.

LaNora froze, poker above her head. She looked at Victoria who lay on her back holding her blood-covered hands over her stomach. Slowly she brought the poker down before rushing to her sister's side.

"Victoria, hold on. I'll get you help. You'll be all right," LaNora said, cradling Victoria in her arms while she knelt in the snow.

"No," Victoria choked.

"You'll see," LaNora said through her tears. "Help is coming."

"No," Victoria repeated and opened her eyes wider as though straining to see.

"We can take the quad."

"Run!" Victoria screamed and then her body went limp.

"No!" LaNora screamed and hugged her friend's lifeless body. Through her tears, LaNora saw a shadow cover her. She turned sharply, releasing her hold on Victoria and looked at the man standing on the other side of the quad with his back toward her.

She frantically looked around for the poker and spotted it at her feet. She reached for it as the man reached up to remove his cracked helmet. Her hand closed around the metal rod and she pulled it to her as she stumbled and scooted away backward.

He removed his helmet and dropped it on the ground. It made a hollow eggshell sound when it hit. Slowly he turned around, searching the ground.

LaNora's mouth dropped open in shock and surprise when she saw his face.

"Mr. Hastings?" she said.

He looked up sharply when he heard her. A smile spread across his thin lips.

"No. Jacobson, Emmett Jacobson. Father to both of the girls you and your friends killed." There was venom in his tone and even with the bit of blood matting the hair on the side of his head, there was a fire in his eyes.

"We didn't kill anyone," LaNora spat back at him. "Ronnie killed herself."

"Liar! She would never do a thing like that," he shouted and continued to search the ground.

"She did because she didn't want to disappoint you. She was going to be sent home," LaNora said, gripping the poker tighter and slowly inching herself up the trunk of a tree until she was standing.

"You and your kind never gave her a chance. She was a special girl." Jacobson's tone softened as he thought of his daughter.

"Is that why you kept her in that room in the attic?" LaNora asked, matching his tone.

Jacobson's head turned sharply toward her. His eyes fixed in an angry glare. "You had no right going into her room," he said through clenched teeth. "Grace told me you went snooping."

"It is a lovely room," LaNora said in a gentler tone hoping to calm him and have him see reason. "I could tell you loved her very much."

"She was my firstborn and light of my life," he said reminiscently. "Her mother was the first to notice she was special. I didn't care. She was my daughter and already special to me. I was proud of everything she did."

"Where is Mrs. Jacobson?"

The corners of Jacobson's mouth pulled downward. His eyebrows became pinched above his nose. "She died after

Grace was born. Grace was so different from my precious Rhonda. She was a tomboy and loved horses. She insisted on painting her bedroom blue and having a western motif." He rocked his head when he said motif as if giving it an air of snobbishness. "She was devastated when she found out what happened to Rhonda. Even at eight years old she vowed to get revenge someday, just as I had."

"I can't imagine what you two have endured," LaNora said, trying to sound empathetic. "Ronnie was a dear friend to me and I still miss her."

"Then why did you kill her!" The fire in Jacobson's eyes returned and the venom in his tone spat from his lips.

"I told you, I didn't. None of us did," LaNora said.

"Your Mother Superior said you were in the room with her when they found her. You tried to hide what you did."

"It wasn't me."

"Liar! You murdered her."

"I was asleep, as were the others. We didn't know until the next morning when Sister Juanita found her."

Jacobson stopped searching the ground when he spotted what he was looking for. He rushed around the quad and swiftly snatched the knife up from the ground at Victoria's feet and clutched the hilt in his hand.

"Mr. Jacobson, why the charade?" LaNora asked. "Why this? Why didn't you go to the police if you thought we murdered your daughter?"

"They didn't believe me. They bought your lies. Thought I was just another grieving parent of a dead child. So Grace and I thought we'd handle it ourselves. But you killed her, too."

"It was a horrible accident. She tried to hit Sister Juanita with a gas can but spilled the fuel all over herself. A spark from the generator ignited the fumes. Sister Juanita tried to save her."

"Lies. Lies. Lies. I thought nuns were supposed to tell the truth."

"I am, Mr. Jacobson," LaNora said indignantly. "If you choose to listen to reason—"

"Enough!" Jacobson screamed. "You're just trying to confuse me. Make me think you're innocent, but we both know you're guilty as sin."

LaNora braced herself. She kept her eyes focused on the knife. While he talked, Jacobson had been bouncing the knife in his hand until he pinched the blade between his index finger and thumb. She was ready when he suddenly drew back and sent the knife spinning through the air toward her. She darted away from the tree just as the blade sunk deep into the tree trunk.

She ran for the pumphouse while Mr. Jacobson went to retrieve his blade. The door to the pumphouse was padlocked shut. The thought of breaking it open with the poker flashed in her mind but she just as quickly decided against it. Had she managed to get inside, she would have been trapped. Instead, she headed deeper into the woods toward Noah's cabin. She would figure out her next move once there.

LaNora reached the cabin but Jacobson had already gained ground. He was too close for her to stop running to open the door so she ran for the driveway. At least in the clearing, away from the trees, she could swing the poker at him again.

The sound of a police siren could be heard as LaNora reached the flat surface of the gravel driveway. She continued to run up the middle, her heels sinking through the snow and gaining traction from the rocks beneath. Without looking back, she could feel Jacobson gaining on her. The sirens drew closer. Help was coming. Her lungs burned from the cold and her legs began to weaken. She forced herself to keep going.

As she rounded a small bend, two SUVs with flashing light bars came to a skidding stop. The driver's door opened on the lead vehicle and an officer stepped out brandishing his pistol. He aimed it at LaNora. "Umatilla County Sheriff, freeze," he yelled.

LaNora stopped and dropped the poker while she put her hands in the air. She opened her mouth to call out to the deputy but her body was suddenly paralyzed by a burst of pain. She was thrown forward to the ground. The sound of a gunshot echoed through the hills and trees and then everything went dark.

CHAPTER FOURTEEN

The first thing LaNora was aware of was a rhythmic beeping sound that came through the darkness. Her eyelids fluttered and then slowly began to open. It took a moment for her mind to process what she was seeing.

"Sisters, she's waking up," a woman's voice said.

LaNora turned her head. A glowing figure in white was standing beside her. Around her head was a golden halo.

"N-n-n-no!" LaNora said and scooted away from the figure until her shoulder hit something solid that stopped her.

"It's okay," the angelic voice said. "You're safe now. You're in St. Anthony's hospital."

Suddenly LaNora's mind caught up with her sight. The white figure transformed a nurse in light blue scrubs. Her halo was only her blonde hair pulled back in a ponytail. She smiled at LaNora with sympathetic eyes. LaNora felt her fear ebb.

Sharp pain in her right shoulder gripped her. She cringed and let out a soft moan.

"Easy, try not to move around. If you need to, I'll help."

"How? What?" LaNora said.

"You were brought in yesterday with a nasty knife wound to your shoulder. The doctors fixed you up and you should be fine in a few days."

LaNora looked around the small room. Bags of fluid with tubes that passed through monitors before being attached to her arm sat on either side of the bed, across the room an empty chair sat by a large tray with a pitcher and cup. It all began to make sense to her.

"Where are the others?" she asked.

"Others?" the nurse said and looked confused.

"My sisters."

"Oh, we notified our local convent. The Mother Superior will be coming by later today to check on you."

"No, you said sisters when I was waking up. . ."

The nurse looked confused but smiled. "No. I'm sorry. I said doctors. I was telling your doctors you were waking up."

LaNora looked around again but saw no one. "Where are they?"

"They'll be right in."

"Oh," LaNora said. "What about Victoria?"

Again, the nurse looked puzzled. "Victoria?"

"Sister Victoria, she was with me."

"There was no one with you when you were brought in."

The image of Victoria lying lifeless in the snow flashed in LaNora's memory causing her to gasp. She turned away from the nurse as her eyes filled with tears.

"It's all right, Sister," the nurse said, trying to console her. "You're safe and on the mend, that's what matters."

LaNora looked at the nurse again. "What about Noa— Mr. Talbot? Is he here?"

The nurse smiled sympathetically. "I'm afraid not. Like I said, you were brought in alone."

A knock on the door caused LaNora to look. A sheriff's deputy, his hat in his hands, filled the doorway.

"Excuse me," he whispered with a deep but gentle

voice. "I just wanted to stop by and see how the Sister was doing."

"She just woke up," the nurse said.

"I see." He looked a LaNora and smiled. "You're lucky to be alive. If your Mother Superior hadn't called us, we wouldn't have gone out there when we did."

"Mother Abbess called you?" LaNora asked.

"Yes." He nodded and stepped into the room. "She said after you and the others had gone, she ran into a street beggar in Portland, a Mr. Drummond. He told her he was hired to play the part of an attorney by a man named Emmett Jacobson. It took us a while to figure out where you were since we had so little information to go on."

"What about Mr. Talbot?"

The deputy lowered his head but looked at her. "Was he the one who lived in the cabin by the woodpiles?"

"Yes. Did you find him?"

"We found him behind his cabin. He was in pretty bad shape. The doctors are doing everything they can for him but they told me he could go either way."

"I can check with his doctor and see if it's okay for you to visit him," the nurse said to LaNora.

LaNora heard the words of her prayer ringing in her ears. *I promise I'll keep my vow. I won't leave the Abbey. Just let him be alive.*

"No. No, it's best that I don't," she said and turned her head away from her visitor and the nurse as tears ran down her cheeks.

"It's okay," the nurse said and gently touched LaNora's hand.

There was a commotion followed by the sound of hurried footsteps in the hall outside. LaNora turned and looked past the nurse and officer. Abbess Claire rushed into the room followed closely by two other sisters.

"Sister LaNora," Abbess Claire said. "Oh, praise the Lord you're alive."

"Mother?" LaNora said and sat up, ignoring the pain in her shoulder. She grabbed Abbess Claire and wrapped her arms around her. "They're all dead," she said and wept.

"There, there, child," Abbess Claire said, gently laying LaNora back down. "Don't be sad. They are with God, now. You're safe." She looked at the deputy. "Did you arrest the man responsible?"

"I'm afraid, he's dead, Sister."

"May God have mercy on his soul," she said. The other two nuns made the sign of the cross and bowed their heads momentarily.

"Child, what is it?" Mother Abbess asked, stoking LaNora's hair and holding her while she wept.

"I-I, I need, I need—" LaNora was weeping so hard she couldn't catch her breath. She sat back and looked at her superior. Her cheeks glistened from her tears.

"Hush, hush. There will be plenty of time to talk, later. Right now, you need to focus on getting better so we can take you home."

"Yes," LaNora said. She turned her head and looked out the window behind Abbess Claire. "Home."

ABOUT THE AUTHOR

A. M. Huff's love for writing began when he was a teenager in a seminary boarding high school. He began writing stories for his own enjoyment, for his eyes only but dreamt of someday becoming a published author. That dream came true in 1998 when he published his first novel, *Secrets*.

Over the years he thought about the stories he wrote back in those high school days and the ones that never quite made it to the page. Pulling from them after 45 years, he completed his latest novel, *And Then There Were Nun*.

Mr. Huff currently lives in Central Oregon and is a longtime member of the authors' group Northwest Independent Writers Association.

For more about Mr. Huff visit his webpage at www.amhuff.com.

Made in the USA
Monee, IL
01 February 2020

21157759R10128